"You're thinking of an en suite bathroom, aren't you?"

She'd refused to turn around when he'd initially spoken, because every single time her eyes connected with that big, hard body, her pulse did stupid things. It was infuriating!

For the last eight months, she'd been indifferent to men, and she wanted it to stay that way. Why now? And why Zach?

"But do we have the time?" she forced out.

Why did her stupid hormones have to come out of hibernation *now*? She rubbed a hand over her face. It *had* to be the location. This gorgeous old villa was the epitome of romance, and they were in Greece...on a Greek island. And the sun was shining and the view out of every window stole her breath. The romance of it all had gone to her head.

Together they measured the cupboard and discussed water pipes, waterproofing, time frames. He moved with a lean-hipped economy that held her spellbound.

So stop looking at him!

Wise advice. But hard to follow. One thing she knew for sure, though—she shouldn't be thinking about sexy times on a Greek island with her hot bodyguard.

T0112729

Dear Reader,

I love devising devilish ways of throwing my heroes and heroines together, creating situations where they can't avoid each other. Forced proximity can make everything so much more...intense. So I'll admit I chortled with glee when I came up with the idea of throwing Janie and Zach together on the set of a reality TV show.

I don't watch a lot of reality TV, but I do have a weakness for a good renovation show. Who doesn't enjoy watching an ugly duckling emerge into a beautiful swan? And in a lot of ways, that's the same journey both Janie and Zach go on, too. Janie's self-confidence has recently been badly shaken, while Zach is haunted by demons from his past. Over the course of the story, though, they both come to realize their own and each other's true worth.

This is a story of hope and self-belief...and love. I hope you enjoy the adventures that Janie and Zach embark upon, and that their journey leaves you feeling as warm and happy as a summer's day in Corfu.

Hugs,

Michelle

TEMPTED BY HER GREEK ISLAND BODYGUARD

MICHELLE DOUGLAS

Harlequin

ROMANCE

Harlequin®
ROMANCE

ISBN-13: 978-1-335-21603-8

Tempted by Her Greek Island Bodyguard

Copyright © 2024 by Michelle Douglas

Harlequin Enterprises ULC
22 Adelaide St. West, 41st Floor
Toronto, Ontario M5H 4E3, Canada
www.Harlequin.com

Printed in U.S.A.

Michelle Douglas has been writing for Harlequin since 2007 and believes she has the best job in the world. She lives in a leafy suburb of Newcastle, on Australia's east coast, with her own romantic hero, a house full of dust and books, and an eclectic collection of '60s and '70s vinyl. She loves to hear from readers and can be contacted via her website, michelle-douglas.com.

Books by Michelle Douglas

Harlequin Romance

One Summer in Italy

Unbuttoning the Tuscan Tycoon
Cinderella's Secret Fling

One Year to Wed

Claiming His Billion-Dollar Bride

Secret Billionaire on Her Doorstep
Billionaire's Road Trip to Forever
Cinderella and the Brooding Billionaire
Escape with Her Greek Tycoon
Wedding Date in Malaysia
Reclusive Millionaire's Mistletoe Miracle
Waking Up Married to the Billionaire

Visit the Author Profile page
at Harlequin.com for more titles.

To my splendid book group: Gerda, Alex, Deb, Janet (Epi), Janet (Hemm), Trisha, Anne, Gwenda and Lucy (not to mention all of our past members). A huge thank you for all of the books we've read together over the years, for the discussions and laughter... and the red wine. Looking forward to our future reading lists, spirited opinions and laughter.

CHAPTER ONE

ZACH'S FINGERS TIGHTENED around his phone. 'What the hell, Sarge? *No!*'

'Too late, soldier.'

Gray, Zach's ex-sergeant from the elite squad he'd served with for eight years, actually used his sergeant's voice. *His sergeant's voice.* Even though when Zach, Gray and Logan had left the army they'd agreed they were equal partners in the business they'd formed—Sentry Protective Services.

His nostrils flared. 'You're not putting me out to grass yet.' He was still in his prime. He thrust out his jaw. Forty-four was still one's prime.

As long as he didn't dwell too much on how his knee ached after completing the army obstacle course he used for training. Or how his muscles ached for days and the bruises took longer to fade after a bout in the ring with Logan.

He could still run a mile in under seven minutes. He could do a hundred sit-ups followed by a hundred push-ups without breaking a sweat. He was a lean, mean fighting machine, thank you very much.

'I'm not ready to retire,' he barked into his phone.

'I'm not talking about retirement, Zach. I'm talking about you stepping up and taking on a more managerial role in the company.'

He gritted his teeth. 'I'm not ready to retire from *the field*. I'm not a darn pen-pusher.'

'Then it's about time you damn well became one!'

He blinked.

'Damn it, Zach, I'm not getting any younger.'

Two damns in as many sentences. Zach's senses went on high alert.

'We need a succession plan.'

What on earth...? 'You're not sixty yet!'

'And you need to loosen the reins and start letting Brett and Francine head up some of the assignments.'

Brett and Francine? They were kids!

He opened his mouth, but before he could speak Sarge barrelled on. 'Hell, Zach, you need to get a life soon or it'll be too late.'

Too late for what?

His back molars ground together. 'I have a life, thank you very much.'

'Work isn't a life—it's a poor substitute for one. Age is supposed to bring wisdom, but you keep burying your head in the sand. It's time to stop.

And if you won't see sense on this then you and Logan can buy me out.'

His head rocked back, his mind racing. Sarge had been due a physical this week. Had he had bad news? Cold sweat bathed his neck. The man was the closest thing he had to a father. He moistened his lips. 'Look, Sarge—'

'I *need* you to take this assignment, it's important to the business. There's no one else who can do it. They're expecting you in thirty minutes.' He repeated the address. 'Be there.'

The line went dead.

Striding out into a crowded London street, Zach hailed a cab, gave the Knightsbridge address to the driver and immediately rang Logan, swearing when the call went to voicemail. He didn't leave a message, didn't know how to verbalise the fears chasing through his mind.

Twenty minutes later he found himself alone in a ground floor room—a library—in one of Knightsbridge's mansions, waiting to speak to the client. His phone vibrated in his pocket. *Logan*.

Striding across to the window to stare out at the massive green square with its immaculate rose garden and towering maple trees, he lifted the phone to his ear. 'Logan.'

'What's up?'

'Did Sarge get a bad report on his physical?'

A heartbeat of silence sounded. 'Not that I know about. Why?'

'Because he's pulled me off the South American job for a domestic assignment—*a dolly assignment*.' He ground his teeth together so hard he started to shake. He was supposed to be shadowing a South American diplomat who a local militia group were targeting. It was the kind of job that demanded his all—every skill, every instinct, every nerve. The kind of job he loved.

Air whistled down the line. 'Pulled rank, huh? Interesting. And Zach, unclench your jaw. You're going to break a tooth.'

That was the problem when you worked with people who knew you so well. They *knew* you.

'Tell me what he said.'

He repeated the conversation.

'Look, you know he's been wanting you to bone up on other aspects of the business—'

'But—'

'And it makes sense. What if one of us gets sick or injured? The others are going to have to step up. You've avoided the management side of things for long enough. I'm with Sarge on this one.'

It took force of will not to clench his jaw again. 'We always knew where my skills lay. I made no secret of it.'

'Well, maybe it's time to upskill, buddy. Prove the old adage wrong, prove that you can teach an old dog new tricks.'

He wasn't *old*!

'How can you train others for what you call a

dolly assignment when you never take one on? You know they're our bread and butter. They bring in the money.'

True, but—

'And you're going to have to do this for Sarge. You know that, right?'

That was the kicker. He *was* going to have to do this.

'Don't worry, I'm toeing the line. I'm about to meet with the client.'

'I'll find out what I can about the physical. What job has he put you on?'

His nose curled. 'Apparently I have to babysit some pampered little daddy's girl while she swans around some frivolous socialite scene spending a fortune on hats and shoes while throwing the odd penny to some unnecessary charity or other.' He had visions of endless garden parties and black-tie events and—

Oh, God. 'Just kill me now.'

Logan's laugh hooted down the line. 'You watch your back, mate. From all accounts those society madams can be deadly. Which daddy's little girl in particular?'

'Plain Jane.'

He used the press moniker without thinking. Because he was still incensed at being pulled from the South American job. And as a displacement activity, because beneath everything ran a deep fear that all was not well with Sarge, and if anything happened to the older man...

The delicate sound of a throat clearing in the doorway had him swinging around. He froze. He'd have cursed except his throat had seized up.

Jane Tierney stood in the doorway, one delicate eyebrow arched. And seeing her for the first time with his own eyes, rather than via random photographs splashed across the papers, *plain* wasn't the first word that came to Zach's mind.

She hip-swayed into the room. 'I'll wear the daddy's girl comment, and I'll own to many attempts at swanning—which I almost have down pat, thanks for asking—but I draw the line at *unnecessary* charities.' Turning to survey him once more, she sank to the sofa and crossed remarkably shapely legs. 'And, just so you know, I don't like hats.'

Logan swore at the other end of the line, clearly hearing her words too. 'You smooth this over and make it right, Zach. Her father has influence—a lot of influence. Don't mess this up for us.'

'Roger that.' He stuffed his phone in his pocket and tried to formulate an appropriate apology.

She leaned back, for all the world as composed as a queen. 'Mr Cartwright, I presume?' She had a voice like warm honey and sin, and soft caramel eyes that momentarily danced.

He swallowed and nodded, resisting the urge

to run a finger around his collar. She deserved an apology and he needed to make it good.

The laughter melted from her eyes and while he hadn't thought a smile graced her lips, it melted from them as well. She folded her hands in her lap—the fingers long, the nails short and square. 'The Plain Jane comment, though, should've been beneath you.'

He dragged a hand down his face. It *really* should've been.

'I'm sorry, Ms Tierney. That was inexcusable. I was angry about something totally unrelated to you.'

'Except for the fact that you apparently now have to babysit me.'

Fighting a wince, he forged on. 'And worried about someone I care about.'

'Sarge?'

How long had she been standing there?

'I directed all of that at you, unfairly. Just… venting. But none of that changes the fact that I shouldn't have said it.'

She blinked.

'I'm truly sorry. I hope you'll accept my apology and let me start again.'

Sarge had said this job meant a lot to them— so it meant a lot to *him*. Zach couldn't mess it up. If he did, he'd never convince the older man that he hadn't sabotaged the assignment on purpose. His hands clenched. He might be as stubborn as his partners accused him of being, but he wasn't selfish. At least, he hoped he wasn't.

Jane Tierney stared at his clenched hands and a frown marred the smooth skin between her eyes.

'I'm appalled at my lack of professionalism. It won't happen again, I swear.'

She leaned back, her shoulders loosening. 'Oddly enough, I believe you.'

A pent-up breath eased out of him. Jane Tierney was the daughter of music legend Joey Walter and lauded actress Colleen Clements. Those two, while no longer married, were rarely out of the papers. To call this family high-profile was an understatement. Their daughter mightn't court the media but she had no hope of avoiding it, no matter how much of a low profile she tried to keep.

'Very well, you're forgiven.'

He almost collapsed at the relief and a devilish dimple appeared in one of her cheeks and it made him think she'd deliberately drawn out his punishment to make him suffer.

If that were the case, it was no more than he deserved. But things inside him sharpened. He'd now need to keep a close eye on her. Not everyone he worked with reconciled themselves to the need for a bodyguard. And if he was being thrust on her against her will, she might try and give him the slip at every available opportunity.

She might not be in any actual danger, hiring him might be a precautionary measure as it was in ninety-five percent of these cases, but he had every intention of treating the assignment as seriously as any other.

A low laugh hauled him back. 'Your face is very easy to read, Mr Cartwright.'

'I make no apology for that. Reading my face could save your life. And please, call me Zach.'

Those shapely brows lifted. 'Well, let me put your mind at rest and assure you I've no intention of being uncooperative. Please, take a seat.'

He took the seat she indicated.

'As you can imagine, this isn't the first time my life has been threatened.'

He detested men who used violence as a weapon against women. And children. Loathed them. Men like his father, who'd used his fists to get his own way, to punish the voicing of a different opinion, or just because he'd felt the need to blow off steam. Men who took pride in the bruises they placed on the bodies of their wives and children, who laughed for days afterwards when they saw the welts and discolouring and said things like 'Serves you right' and 'You'll think twice before you open your mouth next time'. He'd love to rid the world of all such men.

'Heavens! I expect that expression might keep me safe too.'

Her eyes had gone wide and he shook himself back into the present, buried the vicious memories.

'Ms Tierney, what's different about these particular threats? Why would you call in Sentry rather than have your own team deal with it?'

Her nose wrinkled. It definitely wasn't plain. It was kind of cute. And while the face it graced might not be considered conventionally beautiful, it was…

Sweet?

Full of character?

Sexy. The word whispered through him, making things inside him clench in unfamiliar ways. His blood heated and a pulse in his throat burst to life.

'What the hell are the press thinking?' he burst out. 'You—' he pointed a finger at her '—are *not* plain.'

He looked as startled by his words as she was, and Janie didn't know whether to laugh or not.

The way he looked at her had things inside her melting.

Oh, stop it!

She didn't have time for such nonsense. Or patience for it either. After Sebastian, melting over any man was well and truly off the agenda.

Thoughts of Sebastian had acid churning in her stomach. The man had played her for a fool. For two years she'd had no idea of his real agenda. Love had made her blind. When she'd found out the truth it had crushed her, had shattered her sense of self-worth and self-esteem. Her self-respect. It had left her feeling as broken and ugly as the thirteen-year-old she'd once been after she'd first heard the tabloids' reprehensible Plain Jane nickname.

She pulled in a breath. She wasn't making that mistake again. She'd learned her lesson. Never again would she give any man the chance to make her feel so small.

So, no melting!

All the self-talk in the world, though, couldn't stop the light in Zach Cartwright's eyes from making her heart hammer. She'd been shocked at the size of him—a tall, broad man mountain. He wasn't one of those loose-limbed big guys either, but bristling with… She bit back a sigh. Currently he was bristling with irritation.

Not fabulous.

'When placed beside my parents, Mr Cart—'

Blue eyes narrowed.

'Zach,' she hastily amended. She needed this man to stop being irritated with her. She needed him to not make her job harder. 'The fact is, beside my parents most people look plain.'

He dipped his head. 'There's probably something in that.'

Of course there was. If there was anyone who was an expert on the subject, it was her. Not that she resented them for it.

'People are always surprised when they meet me in the flesh.'

He didn't move a muscle, but she felt his wince. She winced too. She hadn't meant him to take it personally.

'As one esteemed member of the press told me—' she affected a cockney accent '—you're not a dog's dinner, miss, but it's the angles, you see. The camera just doesn't love you.'

She watched, fascinated, as one large hand clenched. 'If I hear anyone speak to you like that, I'll deck them.'

'You most certainly will not!' She shot to her feet. 'As my undercover bodyguard, I need you to be low-key and blend into the background.'

He stood too. 'Undercover?'

She bit back a sigh. He didn't know?

'With your height, that's going to be hard to pull off, though, isn't it?'

His nostrils flared as if she'd wounded his professional pride. 'I'm very good at my job, Ms Tierney. If I need to blend in then that's exactly what I'll do. And I'll do it well.'

This man would always stand out in the crowd. *Always.* And she should probably tell him to call her Janie, but… She recalled the words he'd spat into his phone and had to stop her shoulders from inching up towards her ears. He didn't want to be here. He'd made that abundantly, if unintentionally, clear. She either had to get him onside or get rid of him.

She moved a step closer, peered up into his face. 'What does my father have on you?'

Those compelling eyes narrowed again. 'What do you mean?'

'My father is many things, Mr Cartwright.' He opened his mouth, but she held up her hand. 'I know you prefer Zach, but Mr Cartwright just rolls off the tongue. I enjoy saying it. And it still feels friendly, while being more respectful than Zach.'

One side of his mouth kicked upwards. 'Whatever turns you on, Ms Tierney.'

If she'd been drinking anything she would've choked, but then noted the teasing light in his eyes and had to bite back a grin.

'Your father is many things?' he prompted.

'And where I'm concerned, one of those things is overprotective.'

'I'm reliably informed that's a fault of many fathers.'

She digested that in silence. His father hadn't been like that? 'If my father has a weak spot, it's me. The thought of me being harmed is his worst nightmare.'

'And again, I'd say—'

'Yes, yes, I know. But most fathers don't have the money, power or reach of Joey Walter "King of Crooners" Tierney.'

'Ah.' Big hands rested against lean hips and just for a moment Janie found herself bombarded with unbidden—*forbidden*—images.

Her mouth went dry. Recent events had proven to her how *wrong* she could be about a man, and that begged the question: What else in her life had she been wrong about? She needed to keep a clear head. She wasn't letting hormones get in the way of all she needed to achieve.

Not when she had so *much* to achieve.

Strolling away a few paces to put some much-needed distance between herself and Zach's overpowering physicality, she turned and spread her hands. 'When his baby chick is threatened...'

He didn't say anything. He didn't even move—not so much as a flicker of an eyelash.

Fine, she'd spell it out. 'Joey Walter will do whatever he deems necessary to keep me safe—and happy,' she added because her father hadn't crossed that line yet. 'You clearly don't want to be here. So what I'm wondering is how has my father convinced you to take on this job?'

Those blue eyes shifted from the middle distance back to her. 'I've had no communication with your father so far.'

'So it's your boss then.'

'Business partner.'

'What does my father have on your business partner?'

'I've no idea. Hopefully, nothing. But if he does, I'm going to find out what it is.'

The way he said it had gooseflesh breaking out

on her arms. 'You don't know much about this job yet, do you?'

'No.'

No explanation accompanied the single word. He was cagey. In other circumstances she'd consider that an asset.

'Well, you're about to find out as there's a strategy meeting starting in—' she glanced at her watch and swore '—two minutes. I was hoping to fill you in on most of it myself, but we were side-tracked. We'd better head up to the boardroom. And we'd better get a move on.'

'Your house has a boardroom?'

'Tut-tut, Mr Cartwright, this is a complex—an entity unto itself—not a house.'

She led him up the stairs and took the corridor to the left in the direction of her father's business centre. Halting several feet short of the door, she swung around. Before she'd thought better of it, she seized his forearms. 'Can I ask you a favour?'

His brow pleated. 'Of course.'

The corded flesh beneath her fingertips pulsed with heat and power, immediately sensitising her to the fact that this was a hot-blooded man— an *attractive* hot-blooded man—who she was currently manhandling. She snatched her hands away.

His frown deepened. He leaned close until his lips were only a hair's breadth from her ear. 'Are you in danger here, Jane?'

'Janie,' she automatically corrected. Closing her eyes, she hauled in a breath and tried to control her runaway pulse. The man was simply doing his job. 'No,' she forced out from uncooperative lips. 'At least, nothing a bodyguard would consider a danger.' Or could help her with.

'The favour?'

Straightening her spine, she forced her shoulders back. 'The project I'm about to embark on is really important to me. I don't have time to explain what it is now, but you'll find out soon enough. It's just...' Her hands twisted together. 'If you hate the thought of it, and if you don't think you can do it justice, will you please bow out?'

He dragged a hand down his face. 'If your father is blackmailing my business partner...'

Her stomach churned. His loyalty lay there, not with her. And she couldn't blame him for it, but—

'I promise you, though, that I'll keep you safe.'

'I don't want to be kept safe,' she hissed. 'I want to win!'

Before he could respond, the door flew open and her father stood there, beaming at her. 'I thought I heard voices. You're just in time, just in time.'

She submitted when he pulled her into a bear hug.

'How is my princess this morning?'

'Hi, Dad.' She kissed his cheek and then gestured to the man beside her. 'This is Zach Cartwright.'

Her father's paternal affability fell away as he made a long study of her potential bodyguard, taking his time as he sized him up, noting all of Zach's...potential. Zach, unlike most of the men subjected to her father's scrutiny, stood there unmoving and stared back, not a single emotion crossing his impressive face.

And it hit her in that moment that Zach's face was indeed as impressive as his size. He had regular features—a firm mouth that had an intriguing fullness to the lower lip, a strong square jaw and a nose slightly bent as if it had once been broken, which saved that face from being too pretty, too perfect. Short chestnut hair completed the package. She found herself wondering what that hair would look like if he grew it out a little.

'Well, at least he looks big enough to take a bullet for you, pumpkin.' He didn't offer to shake Zach's hand, but turned and headed back into the boardroom.

Janie rolled her eyes. 'Zach also has a sense of humour, which I consider a necessity in a bodyguard,' she called after him.

Just for a moment, blue eyes flashed with humour and Janie thought Zach might actually grin, but it was all quickly contained, his face becoming impassive again. This man rarely smiled.

'You can come and sit up here with me, princess.'

Nuh-uh. She wasn't allowing her father to infantilise her in front of all the people gathered in this room. She wanted—needed—Zach to respect her. Instead, she took the next seat on the left at the bottom of the long oval table, gesturing for Zach to take the seat opposite.

Gathered around the table were her father, his two PAs, the head of their own security detail and her usual bodyguard. She didn't know the man beside her, but she caught the look Zach exchanged with him.

The man turned, held out his hand. 'I'm Gray Garrison, Zach's business partner.'

Sarge? She shook it.

'Gray will be coordinating everything from a home base, the location of which, of course, is yet to be decided,' Joey Walter said.

'Before we discuss that...' Janie folded her hands lightly on the table. 'Can we have a sensible discussion about whether this level of security is actually necessary?'

'Pumpkin, if you insist on continuing with this hare-brained scheme, it's absolutely necessary. Non-negotiable.'

'Three things, Father.' Joey Walter's eyes narrowed. He hated it when she called him Father, considered it too formal. 'One, the scheme is not hare-brained. Two, in business meetings you will refer to me as Janie or Jane.'

'Now listen here, pump—'

'Joey Walter!' He hated it even more when she

called him by his name. Their eyes clashed and she was aware of the man opposite taking in this silent battle of wills.

'And three?' her father grumbled.

'Security is not your area of expertise. Let Gray and Zach assess the information, and then we'll listen to their recommendations for the most appropriate action plan.'

Her father merely hmphed and gestured to one of his PAs, who rose and distributed copies of the three threatening letters Janie had so far received. Janie refused her set. She'd read them once. She didn't need to read them again.

She watched Zach as he scanned the letters, his face growing sterner and grimmer. 'These are ugly.'

Ugly and frankly terrifying. She managed to maintain a stiff upper lip. 'The writer has quite an imagination.' The things the author of those letters threatened to do to her were *vile*. Very carefully, she folded her hands on the table. 'And yet threats are made against my father, my mother and me all the time. Should we give these letters more credence than any of the others?'

'We can't ignore the fact that these might have a personal element,' Gray said beside her. 'They might not, but the threats are…unusually specific.'

'I wouldn't want to take that chance either,' Zach agreed.

Not what she wanted to hear. But after a glance at those letters she suppressed a shudder and nodded. 'Okay. As I said, you guys are the experts. So now to my next question.' Joey Walter opened his mouth, but her glare silenced him. She had Zach's and Gray's full attention. 'Is it necessary for someone to actually be on set with me?'

'What do you mean, on set?' Zach leaned towards her, everything about him going on high alert. He drew the eye like a neon-lit billboard. How on earth would they ever convince an audience he wasn't anything other than what he was—a bodyguard?

'My darling daughter,' Joey Walter drawled, 'has agreed to take part in a reality TV show where contestants vie for a million pounds in prize money.'

'To be donated to the charity of their choice,' she inserted.

Zach's jaw tightened. 'And what do you have to do to win this prize money?'

'For *charity*,' she stressed again. She didn't want him forgetting that. 'The show is called *Renovation Revamp: The Resort Brief.*' Which she thought pretty self-explanatory. 'It involves renovating and styling a rundown resort in a glamorous location.' Pulling in a breath, she did what she could to calm the nerves fluttering in her stomach. 'There are six teams, and six different locations.'

'Where's your resort located?'

'It hasn't been decided yet. That happens during the filming of episode one.'

He held the fistful of letters up. 'You're seriously going to go ahead with that after receiving these?'

'Absolutely.' She gestured to herself and her father. 'If we let every threatening letter we receive frighten us we'd never leave the house. I can't live my life that way, Mr Cartwright. I refuse to.'

And she had too much to prove to walk away from this opportunity now.

CHAPTER TWO

ZACH LISTENED IN silence as Aaron, Joey Walter's head of security, outlined the role Zach was expected to play. Across the table, Janie stared at her neatly folded hands, not saying a word.

An ice-cold fist reached inside his chest. Those letters were appalling. And even though he knew that in the majority of cases things rarely escalated into anything more, acid burned in his stomach.

When Aaron's explanation came to an end, he understood why Sarge had chosen him. And it didn't make him any happier about being here.

He glanced at Janie again and something in his chest solidified. 'The police have been informed about the letters?'

Aaron nodded. 'They're investigating.'

What he didn't say, but what they all knew, was that there was very little evidence to go on and until the perpetrator of those threats actually made a move there was zero chance of the police catching him. Or her.

'Why aren't you dealing with it internally?' He ignored Sarge's narrowed glare. 'Using your own team?'

'Our faces are known,' Aaron said. 'We could've hired someone new but…'

They'd have wanted someone they could trust, and working relationships took time to build.

'Sentry have a proven track record. We want the best on this job.'

He, Sarge and Logan had worked hard to gain that reputation. He ought to be proud of it. He *was* proud of it. It didn't stop him wishing himself away to the South American rainforest, though.

He met Sarge's gaze. 'I want Drew, Janie's usual bodyguard, as part of the team.'

Sarge nodded. 'Exactly what I was thinking.'

'Oh, but…' Crestfallen golden eyes lifted.

He raised an eyebrow. 'Problem?'

'It's just Drew and power tools are not friends.' She grimaced in Drew's direction. 'Sorry, but this role requires DIY expertise.'

'It's true. I can make excellent use of them as weapons, but when it comes to using them for the purpose they were designed for…' Drew shook his head. 'It's not just power tools. It's all tools. I'm strong, though. I can lift heavy things, hold them in place for a long time. But Janie is already giving up her builder and it doesn't seem fair to weaken her team even further.'

It hit him in that moment how much Aaron and

Drew *liked* Janie. They respected her father, but they liked her. Interesting.

He pulled his mind back to the problem at hand. Zach was being swapped in for her qualified builder and Janie was trying to maintain a brave face, but the way the light in her eyes had dimmed told its own story.

'You want someone on our detail on the job. Someone the perpetrator will recognise?' Aaron said.

'Surely he's only a perpetrator once he's committed a crime.'

The sharp edge to Janie's words had Zach stiffening. She'd continually stressed that the prize money was for charity... Did he have a bleeding heart on his hands?

He recalled the fire in her eyes when she'd said, *'I want to win!'* She might be a bleeding heart, but she was a fighter too.

He stabbed a finger to the letters in front of him. 'Sending threatening letters like this *is* a crime.'

Swallowing, she glanced away.

Damn it. He shouldn't have been so harsh.

'Will it ease your disappointment if I tell you that I worked in construction for a number of years when I was younger?' Not that he'd had any choice, his father had forced Zach to work part-time in his building company from the age of fourteen. At sixteen he'd been hauled out of school to work for him full-time. 'My father was a builder. I not only recognise the majority of power tools, but know how to use them. And I'm a pretty decent carpenter.'

The light in her eyes brightened a fraction. 'Okay, well, that's something.'

'Nick has some handyman skills,' Drew said. 'We could—'

'He's newly married.' Janie shook her head, her caramel blonde hair bouncing. 'His wife is expecting a baby. He won't want to be away on set for nearly three months.' She tapped a finger to her lips. 'Darren!' Her face cleared. 'He's been renovating his own home.'

Her father stared. 'How do you know all this?'

Her chin lifted. 'How do you not?'

Zach watched another silent battle between the pair. Joey Walter clearly adored his daughter, but a cord of steel ran through the man and Zach wondered what lengths he'd go to in the interests of keeping his daughter safe, what lines he'd cross.

Over the next twenty minutes the larger scale details were thrashed out and then everyone stood to leave. Joey Walter stared down the table at Janie. 'Let me take you to The Ivy for lunch, princess.'

'Sorry, Dad. I've already promised Zach lunch.'

Zach found himself on the receiving end of a stony glare, before Joey Walter swept from the meeting through a door at the far end of the room, his PAs and security team hot on his heels.

Janie turned to him. 'I am actually hoping you're free for lunch, Mr Cartwright.'

The way she said his name! It made him want to grin. Except he wasn't much of a smiler.

'Zach's free for lunch, Ms Tierney,' Sarge said.

Zach glared at his partner. 'Except I need a quick word with Gray first, if that's okay with you, Janie?'

'Of course.'

She noted his glance at the cameras on the opposite wall and hitched her head in the direction of the door. Silently, she led them down the corridor and his gaze caught on the way her hair shone a particular shade of burnished gold when the light caught it.

'If you'd like a private word…'

He nodded. That's exactly what he wanted.

'Then let me suggest the library.'

Perfect.

She halted at the top of the stairs. 'Do you remember the way or would you like me to—'

'I remember perfectly. We'll be fine.'

She glanced at her watch. 'Then shall I meet you down there in fifteen minutes? If you need longer…?'

'Fifteen will be perfect.'

She started up the stairs for the second floor then turned back. 'Might I make a suggestion…? Close the library door behind you.'

Her father had bribed his staff to listen in at doors? He didn't raise the hair of even one eyebrow. 'Thank you.'

'I'll see you in fifteen minutes.' She took the stairs two at a time. 'And I should warn you—' that honeyed voice floated down to curl around him '—that I'm hideously prompt.'

Excellent. So was he.

'Look,' Sarge started as soon as Zach had closed the library door behind them. 'If this is more of the same—you registering your dissatisfaction—'

'Why is this job so important to you?'

Neither man sat. Sarge frowned. 'You know I want to expand this side of the business. If we do a good job on this assignment...'

If *he* did a good job.

'Joey Walter has a lot of sway, a lot of connections. With a single word he can open previously closed doors for us.'

'We've plenty of work coming in from our current client base.'

'I know you don't want to face the thought of no longer taking part in fieldwork, that you love danger and think you're indestructible and can keep doing it for ever. But no matter how fit and healthy you keep yourself, Zach, in another decade your body is going to start betraying you. And that will put you *and* the client in danger.'

But that was another ten years away and—

'And if you and Logan want to be in control

of a thriving business when I retire, and Zach, I do mean to retire, then we need to start diversifying now.'

The thought had him swallowing. He should've realised this sooner. Sarge had taken him and Logan—both lost boys back then—under his wing. He wouldn't want to leave them high and dry. He'd want to make sure their futures, and the future of the company they'd built from scratch, were taken care of and in good shape.

'Logan sees the sense in this and is willing to embrace it. Why are you being so pig-headed?'

Because when he was working in the field he felt alive—more alive than he felt anywhere else. When he was working in the field there was no time to think, no time to let the past intrude, no time for anything else. And the thought that he was going to spend this assignment *building*. That their damn set was going to be a *construction site…*

His stomach churned. *Don't think about that now.*

Sarge's face softened. 'You're going to need to find a sense of purpose in the real world eventually, son.'

Zach rolled his shoulders. In his experience, the real world sucked.

'Now, I trust you recognise why I thought you the right candidate. I have another meeting in an hour, so you'll have to excuse me.'

'Does Joey Walter have something on you?' Zach widened his stance. 'Is he forcing your hand to take this job?' He lifted his chin, aware he was crossing a line. 'Is he blackmailing you?'

Sarge froze. When he turned back, his face had gone full Arctic. Zach refused to show how much it rocked him.

'Even if he was, Private, that would be none of your business.'

He turned and left, his back ramrod straight.

Zach tapped a fist against his mouth. Right. That *hadn't* been a no. Sarge could be stiff-necked, but he usually shot from the hip. Which meant there was an issue. One he didn't want to share with his business partners.

He blinked when Janie appeared in his line of sight. She'd changed into a pair of jeans and a simple cotton top, all of that burnished gold hair caught up in a baseball cap, dark sunglasses perched on her nose and a huge tote hung from her shoulder. She fiddled with the shoulder strap. 'Did you find out what you needed to?'

'Not yet.'

She assessed him for a moment but didn't press, for which he was grateful. 'Ready?'

He wasn't sure what he was agreeing to, but what the heck. 'Sure.'

Janie scanned the interior of the Chelsea pub, noted Beck and Lena on the other side of the room, but the women, as prearranged, pretended not to notice one another.

'Is this your local?'

She selected a table. 'I don't have a local, Mr Cartwright. Apparently, that's not wise.'

His eyes met hers for the briefest of moments. 'It's the same advice I'd give if I was on the Tierney detail.'

Such a small thing, having a local pub, and nobody in her world seemed to think it a sacrifice. Oh, but she dreamed of being able to walk into a place where they knew you and said hello and made your favourite drink without you asking. Resting her chin on her hand, she let herself think about that for a moment, but then realised piercing blue eyes were scrutinising her.

She straightened. 'What can I get you to drink?'

'I'll get—'

'Nonsense. I asked you to lunch. It's my shout. Besides,' she added quickly, 'I want you to check out the people in the pub, while blending into the background.'

He eased back, folded his arms. 'Just a soda, thanks.'

She suppressed a grin. 'You can shout lunch tomorrow.'

His gaze narrowed and her grin broke free. 'Such an expressive face!' She couldn't help laughing. 'Never fear, Mr Cartwright, my purposes are far from nefarious.' And, of course, she'd be paying tomorrow too. This wasn't a date. He was working and she'd cover their expenses.

She didn't explain further, but went to grab their drinks, returning with his soda, half a pint of bitter for herself and the menus.

He nodded to her glass. 'Your drink of choice?'

'Nope, I'm incognito. Or at least trying to be.'

He removed the straw from his soda and took a generous swig. 'Why?'

'You've scanned the room?'

'More comprehensively than you're aware. There are four exits, not including the two windows I could smash if I needed to. There are only half a dozen people here in the snug, but voices tell me there'd be at least another half a dozen in the main bar. There's only one barman, but I can hear kitchen staff, so I'd expect two to four additional staff that we can't see.' He nodded to her beer again. 'What is your drink of choice?'

What would it take to make this man laugh? 'I'm now tempted to sing "I Love Pina Coladas".' Not so much as a smile. Sigh. 'However, in my opinion, a glass of red can't be beaten. Though beer is good too.'

She set her glass down. 'You see the women sitting at the table near the door with the laptop?'

He didn't even glance across. 'Yep.'

On cue, her phone pinged with a message.

You get him for ten weeks? Am pea-green!

Janie typed back, grinning.

Twelve weeks!

The ten weeks of filming and the fortnight leading up to it.

And green looks good on you.

She stuffed her phone back into her tote. 'They're my besties. In a little while, Beck's going to snap a photo of us, so please don't tackle her to the ground and wrest her phone from her.'

'You want to tell me why?'

She pushed a menu at him. 'After we've ordered.'

She tried to guess what he'd choose, and blinked when he opted for the steak and kidney pudding. Comfort food. A far cry from the burger she'd thought he'd settle for.

'What are you having?'

'The grilled fish with a garden salad.'

His nose wrinkled. She ordered.

His lips twitched, though, when the food arrived and he saw her generous side serving of chips. Popping one into her mouth, she shrugged. 'I couldn't resist. But— Oh! Hot!'

She waved her hand in front of her partly open mouth, to try and mitigate the burn. Reaching for her beer, she gulped down a mouthful. When she glanced back up she found Zach's gaze fixed on her mouth, an arrested expression in his eyes. Her stomach coiled over and over on itself. Her toes and the tips of her fingers tingled.

Oh, that wasn't good. She and Beck might joke about her proximity to Mr Smokin' Hot, but she didn't actually want that heat invading her body and she especially didn't want it messing with her mind.

Clearing her throat, she hauled out the magazines she'd stuffed in her bag and smacked them to the table.

He blinked, and she sent him what she hoped was an unconcerned smile. Her pulse, however, refused to behave, doing a weird unsyncopated dance which made her breath stop-start.

Oh, for pity's sake, Janie! Really?

She did what she could to pull herself back into straight lines.

'Homework,' she explained, opening each magazine to the pages she'd marked and fanning them out across the table. 'I've been researching potential options for renovating and styling different kinds of properties.'

'Tell me about the women by the door.'

'The blonde is Beck Seymour. We were at school together and then at design school. Her mother is in banking and her father sits in the House of Lords. They own an extraordinary estate in Surrey, and disapprove of my parents, though they never fail to attend one of Joey Walter's dinner parties when invited. Beck works in graphic

design and is smart, talented and all round brilliant.' She decided to push her luck. 'She's also
currently single if you'd like me to introduce
you...'

As she spoke, he ate. He looked relaxed, but
across the table she sensed the power and energy coiled inside him. 'The brunette is Lena,
who comes from quite a different background,
but does have a long-term boyfriend, so you're
out of luck there, I'm afraid.'

An eyebrow rose and blue eyes turned wintry.
'Tell me about the logic behind the photo.'

Her face heated. He made her feel like a recal-
citrant child. Glancing down, she stabbed a let-
tuce leaf. 'You don't laugh much, do you?'

'Not much call for it in my line of work. People
don't hire me for my sparkling personality but to
keep them safe. I'm very good at that.'

'But—'

'The photo.'

She heaved out a sigh. 'Once the TV programme
airs there's going to be a lot of speculation about
why I've chosen you as my partner on the show.
Especially when I could've had...' *a qualified
builder or architect, sob.* 'The media will try to
find out who you are and how we know each other.
They'll do Internet searches.'

'We'll set up fake social media profiles and a
website that has my name on it et cetera. The team

will have that in hand. You'll be briefed on our cover story once it's been worked out.'

'Don't I get any say in it?'

He blinked as if the question surprised him. One shoulder—deliciously broad—lifted. 'As you pointed out in the meeting, we're the ones with the expertise.'

'Well, I figure a few photos of us together, leaked at strategic intervals, will add veracity to the fact that we know each other.'

'You want us to pretend I'm your boyfriend?'

'No!' Reaching for her beer, she took a careful sip. 'I really don't.'

Something an awful lot like amusement played through his eyes. 'Should I be offended?'

Fact of the matter was she didn't want her name linked romantically with any man's ever again. She wasn't giving any man the smallest opportunity to make her feel bad about herself.

'To feel offended, you'd need to have emotions, and I doubt you trouble yourself with those.'

Her words, snapped out with acid, made him laugh. She stared. Laughing transformed him. The stern lines around his mouth softened, those blue eyes became warm and vibrant, and that mouth…

Stop staring at the mouth.

Swallowing more beer, she strove to cool the heat rising through her, tried to regain the thread of the conversation. 'Except for professional pride. You have a lot of that.'

'I do.' Resting his forearms on the table, he leaned towards her. 'Tell me what story you'd like for our fictional history and I'll take it back to the team.'

Really? She sct up straighter. 'That we're friends? That you work in construction and have a good eye for making over a property?'

'How did we meet?'

A little fizz of excitement shifted through her. She told herself it was the novelty of coming up with a story. 'Mutual friends.'

'And why would someone like you choose a construction worker over an architect or builder?'

'For his muscles,' she teased, but this time he didn't smile back. She shifted, forced herself to focus seriously on the question. 'Because builders are the boss on a job site and they have apprentices and other workers to do the hard labour for them—they're good at what they do but will they have the stamina for doing a lot of the hard work themselves? Besides, *I* want to be the boss.'

'Not bad.'

The praise gave her an odd sense of pride.

Don't be pathetic.

'And you know what? It doesn't seem in the spirit of the show to turn up with ridiculously overqualified people. I want the viewers to feel that maybe they could achieve a renovation like this themselves.'

'That's a load of rubbish.'

Her jaw dropped.

'I saw the expression on your face when you said you wanted to win.'

Yeah, she *really* wanted to win.

'You'd choose a qualified builder over me in a heartbeat if you could.'

Her shoulders drooped. 'Guilty as charged.' A moment later she forced herself to straighten. 'You're the brother of a friend and I owe her a favour. So I'm doing it to help your fledgling building business become better known.'

He finished his food and pushed his plate to one side. 'A version of that could work.'

'I'm expecting all of the contestants will be asked why they chose their partner.'

'Is there much lag time between when we're filmed and when the show airs?'

'Next to none. Welcome to the joys of reality TV.' She blew out a breath. 'And you know what these shows are like. The director will do their level best to dig up dirt to create drama.'

Easing back, Zach studied the golden face in front of him. 'Why would a person in your position put themselves through that?'

She spread her hands. 'What part of *million-pound prize money* didn't you hear?'

He rolled his eyes. 'For the charity of your choice. I know, I know.' Was she after the kudos? Was that it?

'That money could make a significant difference to some people's lives.'

What charity was she so passionate about that she'd—

'And seriously, Zach—' she leaned towards him '—what am I other than a useless waste of space?'

What the hell...?

'According to the papers, I'm a leech living off Daddy's money.'

'Who cares what other people think? Or—'

She stabbed a finger to the table. 'I have my own interior design business that no one knows about. I want that to change. Also, I'm in an incredibly privileged position. If I have the opportunity, I should be doing all I can to make the world a better place.'

'Which is admirable.' And a million pounds really could make a difference. 'But you're going to a lot of trouble—'

He broke off when one of Janie's best buds, the blonde one, started across to the ladies' room. Janie straightened.

'That's our signal. Beck will snap the photo on her way back to her table. And I want it showing us poring over pictures like these ones—' she gestured to the magazines '—as if we're planning what to do once we're on the show.'

Setting her plate to one side, she fanned the magazines out between them. She'd hardly eaten any of her lunch. Reaching across, he plucked the bowl of chips off the plate and placed it in the centre of the magazines and ate one. 'Eat your chips, Janie.'

She ate one too and then pointed. 'Could you build cabinets like those ones?'

He pulled the magazine towards him. 'Yep.' Piece of cake.

They both noticed the moment Beck emerged from the ladies' room and started back towards her table. Janie tensed. He figured, though, that she'd want the photo to look natural. 'You ever knock a wall down with a sledgehammer?'

His question startled a laugh from her. 'No.'

'It's ridiculously satisfying. Do you want to practice that before we do it on national television?'

Her eyes sparkled. 'For real? Do you mean it?'

'Yep.' He leaned over to point to one of the other magazines. 'Which do you like best—that or that?'

She pointed. And then Beck was past and had taken several photos in quick succession and now she and Janie's other bestie packed up their bags and left.

'How many photos were you thinking we needed?'

'I don't know, maybe three or four in different

locations. Tomorrow, I thought we could go to the library.'

'I have a better idea. Why don't we let Beck and Lena off photography duty and I'll get one of the team onto it?'

'Okay.'

They might as well do it right. 'You said the resort locations would be allocated during episode one.'

'Drawn out of a hat. Not a literal hat, but you know what I mean.'

'Do you know the potential locations yet?'

She seized her phone, clicked a few buttons. 'There are several tropical beach resorts, as you'd expect—an island in French Polynesia, one in Australia's Whitsunday Islands and one in Puerto Rico. There's also a Swiss chalet and a gorgeous villa on the Italian Lakes.' She ran a finger down the list and her nose wrinkled. 'Ah, yes, and we have the wild card.' She stuffed her phone back into her bag. 'A surprise location, just to keep us all on our toes.'

He swore silently. 'If you could opt out of one, which would it be?'

'The wild card, simply because I've no idea what to expect, which means I can't start making any plans for it. And after that probably the Italian villa. I mean it's beautiful, but the scale of the rooms…and the associated building regulations. There's less room to manoeuvre with a building like that. It has headache written all over it. I'm hoping for one of the beach resorts.' Leaning her chin in her hand, her eyes went dreamy. For no reason, his mouth went dry. 'So many options for styling. I could really make a mark there.'

Shaking herself, she glanced up, grimaced. 'I'm guessing the wild card will make it hard for your team.'

An absolute nightmare. 'Gray has all the information?'

She nodded.

Good. Sarge would be making contingency plans.

Her head tilted to one side. 'Where do *you* hope we end up?'

Somewhere remote where they'd be able to monitor who came and went. 'French Polynesia or the Whitsundays.'

'They look gorgeous.'

Except thoughts of strolling along the beach with Janie—

He snapped off the image. He needed to keep things professional. He'd never found that difficult before. And this assignment would be no different.

'Wherever we end up, we will keep you safe, Janie.'

'I don't doubt that for a moment.'

Her smile was too bright and he was seized with an unfamiliar desire to pull her into his arms and proffer what comfort he could. Except that wouldn't be professional.

Shooting to his feet, he said, 'We done here?'

'I…uh…sure.'

'Right then, I have work to do. I'll be in touch about arranging photos and knocking down that practice wall.'

She didn't say anything, but he felt the weight of her gaze as he turned and marched out of the door.

CHAPTER THREE

ZACH'S BROWS ROSE. 'You're nervous.'

With his legs stretched out and his shoulders loose, he looked completely at ease. Janie bit back a sigh. Why couldn't she feel like that?

The two of them were seated in one corner of the green room, waiting for the filming of the first episode of *Renovation Revamp* to start. The five other couples were dotted about the room. She'd tried to start up a conversation with Antoine Mackay, a celebrity chef she'd met a few times, but he'd held out one hand like a stop sign, had said, 'Let's not pretend we're friends.'

Zach hadn't shown it, but she'd felt him bristle. Taking his arm, she'd led him to the sofa in the far corner where he'd have a comprehensive view of the room.

'Charming,' he'd muttered.

'He can be. But not today.' Clearly the rivalry from that quarter wasn't going to be of the friendly variety.

She pulled her mind back. 'Why aren't you nervous?'

'I've done tours of duty in war-torn countries. Whatever else this TV show throws at us, there aren't going to be mines or missiles. So yeah, I'm thinking this will be a doddle.'

'A dolly assignment,' she murmured, recalling his words from a fortnight ago. The reminder that he considered this job nothing more than the overreaction of an overprotective father was oddly reassuring.

'You're not going to let me forget that, are you?'

'Actually, I found it rather comforting. I mean, it was rude too, but hey, you didn't know I was standing there and I think we're past that now.' She grinned. 'After all, we've smashed a wall down together with sledgehammers. We're practically best buds!'

He didn't crack so much as a smile.

Actually, smashing the wall down hadn't been as much fun as she'd hoped. Oh, the smashing itself had been but, rather than the quiet affair she'd hoped for, they'd been surrounded by members of his team, and while he'd been perfectly polite and his instructions clear and to the point, there'd been a distance she'd not been able to breach.

Photos had been taken in strategic locations—the design museum, an architect's office, a tile warehouse. Each of those meetings had lasted less than an hour.

What did you expect? That you'd start the show as best friends?

Well, not best friends, obviously. She already had two of those. But it'd help to have a sense of camaraderie with him. Renovating a resort was going to take all her ingenuity, all her reserves of strength, and being able to share a laugh and a joke with someone...

She straightened. With or without it, she *would* win this challenge. She'd do it for Lena. And all the other Lenas out there. The world was a ridiculously unfair place, and she was in the privileged position of being able to help.

And she'd do it for herself. She'd do it to silence Sebastian's sneers and slurs once and for all and prove she wasn't a failure. She *did* have talent. She *wasn't* wrong about that.

'The dolly assignment comment downplayed the level of danger for you?'

She sent him a swift smile. 'Especially when coupled with the babysitting comment.'

He held her gaze and an unfamiliar pulse ticked to life inside her. 'We're taking those threats seriously.'

'I know.'

She didn't just have a bodyguard; she had an entire team on the case. There'd be two team members at the location pretending to be tourists, as well as Sarge, who'd be setting up and monitoring remote cameras. And Darren. She had a lot of people watching her back.

But hearing Zach denigrate this assignment—the scorn in his voice when he'd spoken to his colleague on the phone—had eased the worst of her fears. Her family received threats all the time. These ones might be more graphic than most, but she shouldn't pay them any more heed than she had any of the others she'd received over the years.

'So why the nerves? You must be used to this kind of thing.'

Most people wouldn't believe her but... 'I don't like the limelight, don't like being the centre of attention.'

'Then why put yourself through this?'

She stared down her nose at him.

He rolled his eyes. 'For the million-pound prize money *for the charity of your choice*, which I've been meaning to ask—'

'I tried hiding when I was a teenager.' She kept her voice conversational, but his mockery stung. 'That didn't work out so well for me—I became awkward, started jumping at shadows. I learned then that facing my fears was more constructive.'

He blinked.

'Is that how you face your fears?' she asked. 'By running away from them?'

'I don't run away from danger.'

She gave a soft laugh. 'I don't think danger is something you're afraid of, Zach.'

They were interrupted by the production assistant clapping her hands in the doorway and asking for the couples—Janie preferred to think of them as teams—to follow her out to the set.

It was a closed set, thankfully, but the lights were bright and the cameras rolling and her stomach tightened and her palms grew damp. Zach leaned down to whisper, 'You've got this, Ms Tierney.' She couldn't explain why, but it bolstered her nerves, had some of the tension bleeding from her shoulders.

The host introduced the couples and they each said a few words. She channelled charm, humour and self-deprecation, but without an audience it was hard to gauge if she'd succeeded.

'Perfect,' Zach murmured, so she chose to believe him. Anything to keep the nerves from showing.

It was then time to draw lots to decide in what order they'd draw their locations in an attempt to stretch this out and make it as painful—oops, suspenseful—as possible. They'd agreed beforehand that Zach would draw their number and she their location.

Zach drew out their number, three and five had already been taken, and wrinkled his nose. 'Number four.'

'Disappointed?' Mike, the host, asked.

He gave a lopsided grin and Janie found her heart thump-thumping. He really should do that more.

'I was hoping for number one.'

Everyone laughed.

Antoine, the celebrity chef, drew number two and whooped and cheered and jumped up and down, punching the air like a footballer who'd just scored a goal.

Isobel, an actor from a recent historical drama series, drew out number one. She glanced at the camera, all hauteur and entitlement, and gave an elegant shrug. 'And number one is where I'm going to be at the end of the series too.'

Janie bit back a grin. Clearly, Isobel meant to play the same catty character here as she did on the drama series. Fun!

'We'll see about that,' Antoine challenged.

And Antoine was going for full drama.

'Low-key, hard-working, self-deprecating,' she murmured to Zach.

'We are all over it. We're going to leave these patsies in the dust.'

Isobel got French Polynesia, because of course she did.

Antoine got the Whitsunday Island.

Contestant three drew the Swiss chalet.

And then it was her turn. With a heart that thumped, Janie made her way across to Mike and the huge electronic board with its six squares.

'Are you feeling lucky, Jane Tierney?' Mike hooted.

No, dammit. She was going to get that rotten Italian villa, wasn't she? Dragging in a deep breath, though, she beamed at him. 'I'm here and about to embark on an amazing adventure. How could I not feel lucky?'

A drumroll sounded. 'Behind which square is your dream location, Janie—the place you're going to spend the next ten weeks? Are you ready to change your life and decide your destiny?'

She resisted the urge to roll her eyes. '*So* ready.'

'Which square do you choose?'

She pointed to the middle square on the bottom row and crossed her fingers.

Please let it be Puerto Rico.

More drumrolls sounded, shredding her nerves further. 'And your *Renovation Revamp* destination is…'

Bells and whistles filled the air and streamers flew all around. *What on earth…?*

'Janie, you've chosen the wild card!'

Her smile froze. As soon as she realised, she turned it into a comical grimace. 'Oh, my goodness, I'm so nervous. Put me out of my misery. Where am I going?'

She was made to guess, of course. 'Hawaii? Or… Banff?' She gave what she hoped was a hopeful smile.

Please don't let it be some historic villa where

she'd need to remain true to the character of the building to make the renovation shine. She wanted a blank slate, a place where she could go wild and where her talents would have jaws dropping.

She watched as a pre-recorded reel revealed the wild card location—an historic villa on the picturesque Greek island of Corfu.

'Excited?' the host demanded.

'*So* excited.' She clasped her hands beneath her chin and beamed up at the screen even as her heart sank. 'Look at it. It's beautiful! I can't believe I get to spend the next ten weeks in such a dream location. I told you I was feeling lucky, Mike.'

She moved back to her seat. Antoine smirked. 'Never mind, Janie. You were always toast.'

She ignored him.

Zach leant down and murmured, 'Not good,' in her ear.

'It's an island, though. That's what we want, right?'

'Not the right kind.'

She had no idea what that meant and there was no opportunity to ask as the last two contestants chose their locations, and then it was time for each team to say a few words about the charities they were supporting.

The charities were enough to break your heart. But a cynical part of her couldn't help thinking that the other contestants had chosen theirs for pathos rather than any real commitment to the cause. There was a fight against Third World hunger, and two separate cancer charities—breast cancer and skin cancer. Her two nemeses, which was how she'd started to think of Antoine and Isobel, represented critically ill children with rare diseases and pet rescue charities respectively. Sick kids, and kittens and puppies. She could already see the photo opportunities. And then it was her turn. She didn't doubt that the director had deliberately saved her for last.

Mike sent her a pitying smile. 'And what's your chosen charity, Janie?'

'It's a small charity in London that I've been associated with for over a decade now, and I hope that my time on *Renovation Revamp* will help raise its profile as more people learn about the good it does.'

'It's called Second Chances.' He made a funny face at the camera. 'And what is it, exactly?'

'A prisoner release assistance scheme.'

Mike cleared his throat. 'That seems an *odd* choice.'

Everyone tittered. It took a superhuman effort to keep a pleasant expression on her face. She spoke about the prisoner support programme and how it helped young offenders turn their lives around. 'Not everyone is born with the same advantages I've had. And—'

'As we've all seen in the other charities we've heard about this evening.'

She gritted her teeth at the interruption. She was used to people dismissing the charity. So what if it wasn't popular or pretty? Neither was she.

'Supporting this charity is my chance to do what I can to help make someone else's life a little bit easier.'

'Don't starving children and maltreated animals and cancer sufferers deserve your help too?'

Ordinarily, by this point Zach would've interrupted Mike. Zach had a way of speaking—with soft menace underlaid with steel—that made most men back off. Not Sarge and Logan, but then they weren't most men. The host's constant interruptions and not so subtle belittling of Janie and her charity were appalling. Except...

In this case, Zach happened to agree with him.

What the hell...? He was going to be helping convicted criminals? Over his dead body!

'What the client's politics are is no concern of yours.' Sarge's voice sounded through him. *'We've been hired to do a job, and we're going to do it whether we agree with their views or not.'*

He took a steadying breath. All valid. All true. He was a professional. He needed to let this go.

'And what do you think about this, Zach?'

Janie turned to glance at him and her eyes widened at whatever she saw in his face. *Damn*. He couldn't feed her to the wolves, no matter how much he might loathe her bleeding heart politics.

'I think, Mike, you ought to let Janie speak without constantly interrupting her.'

Mike's head rocked back and he gave an unsteady laugh. 'Oho, we have a white knight among our contestants.'

He did what he could to stop his lips from twisting. That moniker would probably stick now.

Mike gestured for Janie to continue speaking.

'I was just going to say that the charities you just mentioned, Mike, already have a lot of advocates. A lot of important people are already lobbying governments, the medical fraternity, and the public, to fund research. And they're doing a great job. I applaud each and every one of them. As for me, though, I just want to shine a light on a lesser-known problem. It's one…' she flashed a smile directly at the camera that made Zach's heart kick '…that means a lot to me.' She gave another of those self-deprecating laughs that were starting to set Zach's teeth on edge. 'But I guess everyone can now see that for themselves.'

Mike gave a good-natured laugh too. 'And as the series progresses we'll no doubt learn more about the reasons Janie has chosen this particular charity.'

He moved on, and Zach only had to work at keeping his face expressionless for another ten minutes before someone called, 'That's a wrap.'

The camera, sound and lighting crews started packing up their equipment, Mike strode off without speaking to anyone and the contestants started making their way back to the green room.

Janie was the last to slide from her stool and both Isobel and Antoine glared at her as they strode past.

She blew out a breath. 'If looks could kill.' She glanced up at him. 'Any idea why?'

'I'm guessing it's because you stole some of their thunder.'

She blinked at him.

'Well, clearly the actress is going to play the coldblooded ice queen—all chilly entitlement and win at all costs. While that celebrity chef will be throwing arms and temper tantrums all over the place, creating storms in teacups and blaming everyone else for his mistakes. The other three contestants are all low-key, hard-working and self-deprecating.'

'No, no.' She shook her head so hard all of that old-gold hair swished around her shoulders. 'That's us. That's me.'

'Not any more.' They'd stopped walking and stood at the edge of the set. He leaned down until they were eye to eye and pointed back the way they'd come. 'Not after your performance out there, you're not.'

For the briefest of moments her gaze fixed on his mouth. She moistened her lips, the gold flecks in her eyes briefly flaring. He shot upright, chest tight, fingers clenched so hard they ached.

Her throat bobbed. 'What do you mean?'

'Now you're the bleeding heart.'

'The *what*?'

'Naïve, earnest…*misguided.*'

Her eyes narrowed as he spat the last word.

'What the hell kind of charity is that?' He pressed a fist to his brow. 'A prisoner release assistance scheme?' He swore. 'You *can't* be serious.'

He'd never known that gold could turn to ice, but her eyes were rimed with an Arctic chill and she stood straight and tall. Unflinching.

'You're not being paid to have an opinion on the topic.'

Which was both true *and* infuriating.

He stabbed a finger ceilingward. 'Criminals deserve to go to jail.'

'And when they've done their time, they deserve a second chance. They deserve the opportunity to start again and make a new life for themselves. Everyone deserves a second chance, Mr Cartwright.'

Her *Mr Cartwright* didn't sound teasing or friendly or fun. And he couldn't explain why but it was a knife to the heart.

And then a sound came from his right and instinct took over and he immediately moved in front of Janie to block her from view.

The production assistant appeared. 'We wondered where you'd got to.'

She had a phone in one hand and a folder in the other. Things inside him drew tight. How long had she been hovering in the shadows? Why the hell hadn't he been paying more attention?

'Here are your plane tickets, along with all of the other information you need about the rules and the production schedule.'

Janie moved out from behind him to take the folder the assistant held out. 'Thank you.'

'You'll be flying out first thing in the morning. It's an early start, I'm afraid.'

'No problem.'

Janie's voice was all smooth urbanity—no anger, outrage or agitation coloured it. If he hadn't witnessed any of it himself, he'd have been hard pressed to sense it now. Except perhaps in the deepening of the creases at the corners of her eyes as if she was fighting a headache, and the paleness of lips that had been pressed together too hard.

He bit back something between a groan and a growl. Her life was hard enough at the moment. He shouldn't be making it harder.

But... A prisoner assistance scheme? *Seriously?*

He'd witnessed the effects of violent crime— he and his mother had both been victims to it, and the memories of that time made him sick to his stomach. For Pete's sake, one of her father's crazed fans was threatening to do unspeakable things to her. How, for a single moment, could she believe supporting a charity like Second Chances was a good idea?

Pulling his phone from his pocket when they reached the car, he informed Sarge of the resort's location and took photographs of all the documents in the folder and sent them through too.

'Home?' he asked when he was done.

'Yes please.'

She didn't look at him when she spoke and he had to bite back an oath.

'Look, we don't have to agree on political or social issues. All we have to agree on is that I'll do my utmost to keep you safe and my best on set as your builder.'

She swung to him, her eyes flashing. 'I had no idea you were so judgemental, that your world was so black and white.'

He preferred the fire to the ice. 'You haven't seen what I've seen.'

'And you haven't seen what I've seen.' He blinked at her swift retort. 'Are you really so incapable of empathising with other people?'

What the hell...?

'Though I guess empathy isn't a requirement of your job. Maybe it's even an impediment.'

'I can empathise!' he hollered.

His teeth ground together. This woman was starting to get under his skin and that wouldn't do. It wouldn't do *at all*. He didn't allow women to get under his skin. And he was on assignment.

Even if he didn't believe she was in any real danger, he still needed to keep a clear head.

'Well, that's good to know.' She folded her arms. 'Because on this particular social issue, plan to have your views challenged.'

Silently he said, *Yeah, good luck with that.*

As soon as the plane was in the air the next morning Janie handed Zach a copy of the documents that had been in the folder. She'd emailed copies to both him and Sarge as well. He had a printout in his suitcase but he didn't mention that, just let her be efficient.

He was hoping after her snit with him yesterday things between them could get back on an even keel. Somewhere in the back of his mind laughter sounded. *Even?* None of his dealings with this woman could be described as even.

For a brief moment he recalled the pub lunch they'd shared and...

And what? Was he hoping for more of that? *Seriously?* He swatted the thought away. All of Sarge's arguing with him about getting a life was making him soft in the head.

'Why is Corfu not the *right kind of island*? You said an island would be a good location.'

'Corfu is neither small nor remote. It's a big tourist destination. It'll be impossible to monitor everyone who comes and goes.'

He watched her mull that over.

'But we can work with it.' He didn't want her worrying about her safety. He shuffled through the file until he came to the photo of the villa. A three-storey stone building with a semi-circular first-floor balcony. 'So this is what we're working with.'

She traced a finger over the photo. 'This wouldn't have been my first choice.' Her scent rose up all around him—something sweet and restful, a blend of cashmere and violets. 'But it's rather beautiful.'

If your taste ran to rundown and ramshackle.

She glanced up and their gazes locked. The air between them shimmered. 'A Greek island.' She swallowed. 'You ever been?'

Adrenaline flooded his every cell. 'Nope. What's it like?'

'I've never been either.'

She hadn't—

Her gaze snapped away. 'But it's a dream location. So romantic. We need to do it justice for the people watching the show.'

'Why?'

Did she want to win the audience vote?

What was he thinking? *Of course* she wanted to win the audience vote.

'What do you mean, *why*? Where we're going, what we're about to do, that's some people's dream. It should be treated with respect.'

It wasn't his damn dream. He'd give his right arm to be heading to South America right now.

She shook the papers she held. 'Okay, to work. We've the production schedule—the show will air on Sunday nights—and a list of the rooms we'll be making over.'

'Bedroom, bathroom, dining room, reception room, reception foyer, outdoor area…and a mystery challenge tailored individually to each property,' he said, ticking them off.

'You've memorised it.'

'I like to be prepared, and when I'm undercover I take my role seriously. We get a week to renovate each room, but two weeks for the mystery challenge. At the end of each week the judges will inspect the rooms via a video call and give a score out of twenty.'

'And you can go to the top of the class.'

Internally, he smiled. There might now be an undeniable distance between them, but she still had a sense of humour.

She gestured between them. 'You and I can work all the hours we want, but we're only allowed to work our team a max of eight hours a day, as set out in their industrial award.'

'Are you going to work me sixteen hours a day?' He was up for it, but curious to see what she'd say.

'I expect so. After all—' she sent him the sweetest of smiles '—we're representing a very worthy charity.'

He grinned. He couldn't help it. 'Is that my punishment?'

For the briefest of moments her gaze lowered to his mouth, but she dragged it away and shrugged. His heart sounded loud in his ears.

'You said you'd do your best for me.'

'I meant it.'

Working sixteen-hour days sounded like a great idea. If he was working sixteen-hour days he'd be too tired to think about stupid things. Like what it'd be like to kiss Janie Tierney.

He didn't *feel* things for his clients. That was a road leading straight to hell, not to mention personal ruin and devastation. Cold and clinical, vigilant, those were his code words. Janie might be easy on the eye, but he couldn't let it mean anything.

He clenched his jaw. He *wouldn't* let it mean anything.

CHAPTER FOUR

JANIE STARED OUT of the window as their minibus travelled the hour north from Corfu city. The Ionian Sea sparkled sapphire in the morning light, the exact same colour as Zach's eyes. When the road dipped inland they were treated to golden fields, grazing goats and shady olive groves that looked as if they'd been there for centuries.

'It's unbelievably gorgeous,' she murmured.

Beside her, Zach said nothing. A man of few words. Though as she hadn't appreciated the ones he'd blasted at her yesterday, that was probably a blessing.

Despite the heaviness that wanted to settle on her shoulders, the voices whispering in her head that said she'd bitten off more than she could handle and the low-level dread that had weighed heavily in the pit of her stomach since she'd read that first threatening letter... The longer she stared at the view, the lighter she started to feel.

She could do this and she would. To prove her naysayers wrong, and to find herself again. For

Lena and every other person who deserved a second chance. None of them were failures.

'The villa should be just up ahead,' Cullen, the head of their production crew, said, turning the minibus into an overgrown drive that she made a mental note to clear. Overgrown could be picturesque, but this was a jungle.

Her silent laugh had Zach glancing at her. She pretended not to notice. She'd already been far too aware of him on the journey. His big body so close to hers, the intriguing flex and play of muscles when he moved, the way those blue eyes took everything in.

While she wanted him to be vigilant, she didn't want him sensing the ridiculous fantasies plaguing her where he was concerned. As if she was some schoolgirl with a stupid adolescent crush. Except the fantasies chasing through her mind were far from innocent.

And they weren't going to happen! She forced herself to remember how she'd felt when she'd learned the truth about Sebastian. She'd felt small. Stupid. Diminished. No way was she going through that again, or setting herself up for another fall. The only way to prove she wasn't a fool was to stop acting like one.

'Something funny?'

She waved a dismissive hand, eyes glued to the window. 'Just spending our budget already.'

She needed to be careful with the budget,

though. If she overspent they'd be penalised and then everyone would think her a loser who couldn't—

Stop it!

As they broke through the trees she kept her attention on her surroundings rather than the man beside her. They emerged into a clearing and—

Her heart stopped for two-tenths of a second. The view... Oh, the view! *This* was why words like azure and cerulean had been invented because, no matter how hard it tried, the word blue couldn't capture that much beauty.

A sapphire sea spread before them in sun-sparkled splendour, framed by a rocky shoreline, date palms and cypress trees. How had she never known that Corfu and the Ionian Sea was this beautiful?

Only after she'd drunk in her fill did she follow the green lawn up from the pebbly beach to the villa overlooking it. That was when reality hit her right between the eyes. She winced, commending herself for not grimacing, groaning and swearing. Or for bursting into tears.

At some point in its past the villa had been rendered in plaster and painted, but haphazard sections of dirty yellow render had fallen away to expose the stone beneath, leaving it pockmarked and disfigured. It looked decrepit, unloved and unlovely. The alternately weedy and stunted excuse for a garden reflected the same neglect as the building.

Zach stared from it to her and back again. Nobody spoke. Wordlessly, they piled out and stood there staring.

'Is this some kind of joke?'

Zach's demand snapped her out of her daze.

Cullen scratched his head. 'I, uh… It's more rundown than I expected.'

With a frown, she shook her head at Zach. This wasn't Cullen's fault. He hadn't chosen the location. He was just doing his job. Gritting her teeth, she pushed her shoulders back. And so would she.

She'd show *everyone* what she was made of.

'You need to film our arrival, right?'

He sent her a grateful smile, motioned for the crew to set up. 'We'll film the two of you in front of the villa to share your first impressions. Then we'll follow you inside. Today only you and Zach will appear on camera. I won't appear, but viewers will hear my voice when I ask a question or prompt you.'

She knew all of that already, but was grateful for the recap. It gave her a chance to gather her wits and recharge her game face.

'Ready?' At her nod, Cullen called, 'Action.'

Janie turned from viewing the villa to smile at the camera. 'Well, it's a little more rundown than I expected.' She held up their photograph of the villa. 'This looks like it was taken a decade ago, but I'm guessing all of the contestants are going to find themselves in the same boat.'

'Zach?' Cullen prompted.

Zach made a noncommittal noise.

Janie winked at the camera. 'You're going to find that Zach is a man of few words. He's the strong, silent type. I'm emphasising *strong* because we're going to need all your muscles on this job, Zach.'

'And yours.'

'It might not be looking its best at the moment but...' she nudged him '...tell me it has good bones.'

Planting his hands on his hips, he surveyed the villa. The sun glinted off chestnut hair, turning the colour rich and vibrant. The dance of light and shadow against his face—

She dragged her gaze back to the villa, her heart pounding.

'It has good proportions,' he allowed. 'In its heyday it would've been a handsome building.'

And it'd be handsome again. She *could* do this. An old fire ignited inside her.

'This is seriously exciting!' Grabbing Zach's arm, she dragged him in her wake until they were silhouetted against the view. 'Look at that.' She silently screamed at the camera. 'Isn't it beautiful? I know the next ten weeks are going to be challenging, we've a lot of hard work ahead of us, but being able to look at that every day… I can't believe how lucky we are.'

Zach stared as if afraid she'd had too much sun.

She clapped her hands. 'Come on, let's see inside.'

Gloom greeted them as the front door opened and they stepped into a large foyer. A generous staircase arced up to the first floor. Off to the right, a huge room opened out, thick with dust and must. She wrinkled her nose and moved across to the chinks of light showing through huge wooden shutters. Opening the window, she swung a shutter open.

'Let's see if we can let in some light and—' The hinges gave an ominous shriek, Janie jumped as first one hinge and then the other pulled away from the frame and the whole thing clattered to the garden below. With a hand clapped to her mouth, she turned back to the camera, shaking with laughter. 'Right, we'll be fixing the shutters then.'

Moving past her, Zach simply pulled the other shutter from the window frame and eased it to the ground. 'The wood's rotten, but that's an easy fix.' He did the same with the other two sets of shutters.

A light breeze floated through the windows, stirring the dust, making her sneeze. Old tables and chairs, discarded boxes of crockery and cutlery and other assorted odds and ends littered the room. They'd have to clear this, or pay someone else to do it.

'You're both quiet,' Cullen prompted.

'I'm just taking it all in.'

'Does the dirt and grime bother you?'

That had her grinning. No way was she being thrust into the role of pampered princess. 'It's going to get a whole lot dirtier before we're through with it.'

'This could be a great room.' Zach moved across to a wall and rapped his knuckles against it. 'High ceilings, a generous floor space. We've a ceiling rose that needs some work but...'

'The fireplace will be fabulous once we clean it up.' In her mind's eye she could see it crackling away, all cheerful and warm. 'And then there's that view...' She gestured out of the windows. 'We have to find a way to do it justice.'

'What are you seeing?' Cullen prompted.

'Two sofas facing each other here in front of the fireplace...a bookcase on the far wall with a couple of wingback chairs... A writing desk there...'

Zach crouched down, tapped the floor. 'Antique tiles.'

She pointed. 'And a decorative frieze along the top of the wall. This could look so grand!'

Before she was aware of it, she and Zach were throwing around ideas and making plans and she forgot about Cullen and the camera. She only came back to herself when Cullen seized on a brief silence while she and Zach regrouped.

'I think we might wrap it up there.'

Oops. She might've got a little carried away. But it was better than feeling overwhelmed and useless, and a poor ambassador for Second Chances and a failure in general.

'We'll unload your bags and head back to our digs.'

The production crew, along with the other two members of their renovation team, were staying in the nearby village. Only she and Zach would live onsite.

'Here's the building report.' Cullen fished the folder from his bag and handed it to Zach. 'Apparently, someone has given the bedrooms and bathroom set aside for your use a thorough clean. And here are the keys to your hire car, which should be parked around the back. I think that's it. We'll reconvene nine a.m. Monday.'

Today was Saturday.

Their bags and associated equipment were unloaded onto the lawn. No special VIP treatment for them.

Zach turned to her after they'd waved the others off. 'Where do you want to start?'

She folded her arms. 'How about with you telling me why you have such a set against my charity?' She ought to let it go, but it burned and chafed at her. A horrible thought occurred to her.

'Have you or someone you love been a victim of crime?'

His face tightened and he pointed a hard finger at her. 'That's not up for discussion.'

'Shut down, smacked down and stonewalled. Let that be a lesson to you, Plain Jane.'

'Stop calling yourself that!' He gestured to the house. 'Focus on that. *That's* why we're here.'

Biting back a sigh, she shouldered a bag and lifted two of the suitcases. 'Let's take these inside and do a full reconnaissance.'

'I'll carry those.'

Her answer was to stick her nose in the air and start towards the house. 'I am sledgehammer woman! I am strong and invincible.' Also, for the last month she'd been lifting weights—a training of sorts. And while it had made her stronger, it didn't stop the suitcases from being dead weights by the time she got them inside. Dumping them in the foyer with a sigh of relief, she moved down the corridor, glancing into a series of rooms, to eventually emerge into the kitchen at the back. The place looked as if it hadn't been cleaned in years.

'Generous but primitive,' Zach said behind her.

They retraced their steps and headed upstairs. On the first floor there were six bedrooms—none of which had en suite bathrooms. A shorter flight of stairs took them to two smaller bedrooms tucked in the eaves that looked out over an overgrown back garden. As these had their names pinned on the doors, clearly they were the ones put aside for their personal use.

She opened her door and stared. 'I thought Cullen said they'd been cleaned.'

'You can take my room.'

'I'm not afraid of a bit of dust. I know how to use a vacuum cleaner and mop. Besides—' moving past him, she pushed open his bedroom door '—your room isn't any better.'

'Nothing to do with cleanliness, Janie. That room had your name on it. Means someone will be expecting you to sleep in it.'

Fear flickered in her stomach. She did what she could to quash it. Those letters had been sent to scare her. Someone's idea of a sick joke. Nobody was out to get her.

'Probably innocent enough, but my job is to make it harder for anyone to find you where they expect to.'

Of course it was innocent. She refused to start seeing bogeymen behind every door. Hitching up her chin, she moved across to the window. 'They'd need a pretty tall ladder.'

Zach moved to stand beside her, scanned the back garden. 'No pool.'

'And we've neither the time nor the budget to put one in, but a pergola—grapevines hanging from it…a paved courtyard.'

One side of his mouth hooked up and it made her pulse dance. 'A pizza oven?'

'Yes!' She'd research how to build her own pizza oven tonight. 'Come on, let's get these rooms shipshape.'

'I'm going to do a recce outside. And I need to check in with Sarge.'

'Okey-doke. Let's get to it.'

It took her two hours, but eventually the two bedrooms and bathroom had been cleaned to a reasonable standard.

Zach halted when he crossed the threshold of his room. 'You didn't have to clean my room.'

'I saw what you were doing outside.' She shrugged. 'It only seemed fair.'

Zach had found a brush-cutter in one of the back sheds, along with a hedge-trimmer. He'd spent two hours laying waste to the jungle at the back of the house. Both he and Sarge thought the threats empty, didn't expect to see action on this assignment, but Joey Walter was paying a hefty amount to keep Janie safe and Zach was playing this one by the book. He planned to be ready for anything.

And limiting the places where any potential stalkers could hide was one of them. The pine grove out the back was now shady but clear. He'd be able to see anyone loitering out there.

'I can envision little café tables beneath the pines...carafes of something lovely and chilled... condensation forming on glasses.'

Her eyes went dreamy and Zach backed up a step, forced his gaze away.

'Happy chatter and laughter.'

A vivid picture formed in his mind. He could almost imagine himself, beer in hand and legs stretched out at one of those little tables she described, taking it easy.

He shook himself. *Relaxation?* Was he nuts? He loathed being still. And yet he couldn't shake the image.

Janie turned and headed downstairs. He stared after her and frowned, scrubbed a hand through his hair. The woman he'd met at the pub—playful, slightly mischievous—had gone. All of that *vividness* had been replaced with friendly efficiency. He'd thought, when they'd started riffing off each other downstairs, coming up with ideas for the reception room fast and furious, that they'd regained their previous footing.

But nope.

He tried telling himself that this professional distance was wiser. He gritted his teeth. *It was.* Except…

'If you hate the thought of it and don't think you can do it justice, will you please bow out?'

Her words from their first meeting rose in his mind to peck at him. He hadn't promised, not out loud. He'd promised to himself, to Sarge, to keep her safe, that was all, and yet…

Damn it all to hell.

This professional distance would be better for him, but some instinct told him it wouldn't be better for her. Some people needed to like the people they worked with. It helped them concentrate on the work rather than wasting time labouring over how to negotiate a difficult relationship—or what they saw as difficult. They used their energy rehearsing what to say and what not to say, guarding their thoughts and their tongues. He suspected Janie was one of their number.

If he was going to keep the promise he hadn't made, he was going to have to work out a way to win her trust and get her to like him again. How the hell was he supposed to do that? He wasn't good with people. He was good at sensing danger and being vigilant, keeping people safe and making sure the bad guys got their comeuppance.

'What are you doing up there, Zach?' Janie hollered up the stairs. 'We've got a lot to do before the team arrives on Monday.'

They did? He rolled his shoulders. If he did that well enough, maybe it'd earn him a gold star.

He found her in that front reception room. 'Private Cartwright reporting for duty, Captain.' He saluted and clicked his heels together.

Her brows lifted and the corners of that very mobile mouth twitched. It gave him a shot of adrenaline. Odd. Adrenaline usually came from facing danger and thwarting it. No matter how hard he tried, he couldn't view Janie as any kind of threat.

He shook out his arms and legs. 'What's the plan? What do you want done?'

'I want to clear this room and move everything into that smaller reception room off the kitchen. We're not throwing any of it yet—we might need it or use it for staging once the rooms are renovated.'

He glanced around. Something felt off about this room. It was too full of junk as if—

As if that was deliberate. The director's way of saying welcome to *Renovation Revamp*?

'And the kitchen needs a spit and polish because whether it's part of the renovation or not, it's going to be where we cook, where the team keeps their lunches and makes coffee…eats.'

The less time anyone had unsupervised access to his and Janie's sleeping quarters the better. As much as possible, he'd like to keep everyone where he could see them.

He needed locks for those bedrooms. Deadbolts.

'And then I want to go into town.'

'For?'

'Groceries, a late lunch, some additional cleaning products, and to touch base with local suppliers.'

At this rate they might be in bed by midnight. Moving across to a window, he surveyed the view. 'There's a big tree out there, nice and shady. Looks like an oak.'

'Is this you making conversation?'

'I'm a man of few words, remember? I don't make conversation.'

She huffed out a laugh. Another surge of adrenaline sharpened his senses, made him aware of sun sparkling on sapphire water, the way her hair gleamed like tarnished gold even in the dust and grime of the room, the scent of salt in the air.

'I was thinking we could take this table and a few of the chairs out there. It'd make a nice place for the team to sit during break times.'

'That's a great idea!'

They cleared the room of all the big things that required two people to lift, and created a casual eating area outside under the big tree. He nodded when they were done. Everyone would much prefer to eat out here than the kitchen. Mission accomplished.

He turned back to Janie. 'Breakfast was a long time ago. I vote we go into town now and tackle the rest of this when we get back. We'll work better after some food and fun.'

'Fun?'

He might've made her smile once or twice, but he hadn't breached her guard. Not yet.

You could apologise.

But he wasn't sorry about what he had said.

Apologise for the way you said it then.

He widened his stance. 'When we get back we'll divide and conquer. One can keep moving this stuff while the other tackles the kitchen.'

'And bathroom. It's filthy too. And as the team will need to use it…'

Right. 'Whoever finishes first will then help the other. And you can choose.'

'Me?'

'You're the boss.'

She folded her arms. 'You're happy to clean?'

'You learn to keep things shipshape when you're in the army.'

She glanced around. He waited, intrigued to find out which one she'd choose—cleaning or packing.

'It'd be safer if I took the kitchen.'

'You have a cleaning fetish or something? Surely your father employs an army of cleaners.'

Laughter lit those golden eyes. 'I don't *live* with my father, Mr—'

But the Cartwright never came and for some reason it made his heart sink. 'Why not?'

'That's one of those off-the-table topics.'

Interesting. 'Why would the kitchen be safer?'

She pointed to the boxes littering the room. 'I'm dying to see what's inside those, but now is not the time to get distracted.' She gestured towards the kitchen. 'But there's something dead in the oven and I really don't want to deal with it.'

'You go take first shower. I'll deal with the oven.'

'Thank you.'

After showers, they headed out the back to the tradesman's van they'd been allocated. She took one look at the manual gearbox and handed him the keys.

'I'll give you lessons.'

'We won't have time for that.'

'If something happens, you need to be able to drive this thing.'

Her head whipped around. 'If something happens... Like *what*?'

Hell, he'd alarmed her. He kept his voice casual as he started the van. 'Like I fall down the stairs and break a leg.'

Her shoulders loosened, but tensed again a moment later. She pointed at him. 'No falling down the stairs. No broken legs.'

'Roger that. Now, buckle your seatbelt.'

The village was only a five-minute drive away and they ate a hearty lunch of moussaka and bread in a courtyard with a large olive tree. They stuck with drinking water, but he made a note to buy a few bottles of the local wine to keep at the villa.

Sipping a glass of wine at that table under the shady tree, staring at what even he had to admit was an amazing view, might help loosen Janie up, because the food hadn't worked. She didn't make idle chitchat or tease him. She busied herself making a shopping list and researching local suppliers on her phone.

Rolling his shoulders, he shifted on his chair. 'Look, I'm sorry for the way I spoke to you at the end of filming yesterday, okay?'

She started as if she'd been a million miles away. 'Okay.' Eyes the colour of cognac narrowed. 'But you're not sorry for what you said.'

'I'm sorry I expressed myself so...'

'Rudely?'

'Forcefully.'

That infuriatingly mobile mouth pursed. 'And yet the reason why you're so opposed to my charity is off the table, not open for discussion.'

He had no intention of telling her the real reason he hated her charity. 'Criminals should be punished,' he ground out.

'And jail isn't punishment enough?'

'These are people who have made seriously bad choices. They need to understand there are ramifications for that.'

'I'd have thought jail was a pretty big ramification.'

He slammed a finger to the table. 'Violence should *not* be rewarded.'

Two beats of silence passed. 'Not all criminals are violent, Zach.'

She stared at him, her eyes going dark and troubled, her teeth gnawing on her bottom lip. He wanted to tell her to stop that, that she'd do herself an injury. But the longer he stared the greater the hunger that ballooned in his chest. It grew so big it blocked his throat.

'You were a victim of a violent crime,' she said quietly.

The soft words knocked it free with the force of a punch. *What the...?*

Her brow pleated. 'Heck, Zach! The person who'd get the better of you had to be a giant or—'

She broke off, her face falling and going sort of soft in a way that had things inside him melting and jerking and roiling.

'You were a child,' she whispered. 'Someone bad hurt you when you were a child. Oh, Zach...' Her hand lifted and for a moment he thought she meant to reach across the table and touch him. He told himself he was glad when she didn't. 'I'm sorry that happened to you.'

What the hell?

'I haven't said a damn thing!' But an old pain he'd never been able to extinguish burned and throbbed. 'How can you go from that Point A to that particular Point B on absolutely nothing?'

'Your face. I keep telling you it's expressive.'

It damn well wasn't. It was only expressive when he wanted it to be.

'Look, we're never going to agree on this charity of yours, so—'

'You're saying you refuse to even hear my reasons for supporting Second Chances?'

He didn't want to hear her reasons.

'I'm saying that despite our opposing views on that topic, I'm planning to do my best for you on this project. I promise to neither undermine nor sabotage you.'

'I never thought you would.'

'And now we're going to the hardware store.' He stood. This conversation was well and truly over.

CHAPTER FIVE

On Monday they started work for real. Not that they'd done anything else since arriving. But this time the camera was rolling.

Their first assignment—to makeover a bedroom.

Janie chose the big double bedroom on the first floor with its French windows out onto the circular balcony and sweeping views of the sea. Breathtaking. Not only was it the largest of the bedrooms but it was also the one that needed the most work. But as far as she was concerned they might as well go big or go home. She had a reputation to establish.

Window and door frames needed replacing and the floorboards were in desperate need of sanding. Plaster needed fixing and the wood panelling on one wall had rotted. Pulling several boards off, though, and she saw the potential of the underlying stone as a feature wall. She bounced from foot to foot. This room could look fabulous!

One glance at the grim set of Zach's mouth,

though, had her stomach plummeting. He didn't want to be here. He might've promised he'd do his best but it didn't change the fact that he loathed everything about this assignment. She needed to find a way to get him onboard.

Out on the lawn, circular saws cut through the air. Pulling the rotted wood from that wall, she went over her and Zach's previous conversations. She needed to find a way to help him not hate this job.

I'm a pretty decent carpenter.

She paused. The way he'd said that… Maybe—

'Everything okay?'

Zach measured the inside doorframe, a toolbelt fastened around his hips. A sigh rose through her. What was it about a man and a toolbelt?

Ha! Both Darren and Tian were wearing toolbelts but she hardly noticed them.

'Janie?'

She looked back at him.

I'm a pretty decent carpenter.

'Zach, could you build me a bed?'

'What kind of bed?'

Seizing her sketchbook, she made a sketch of a four-poster bed—a light, airy concoction she could swathe with delicate, floaty drapes. Darren and Tian, carrying in the freshly cut window frames, glanced over her shoulder as they passed. All three men shrugged.

She blew out a breath. Where was their enthusiasm? 'Okay, guys, look. You might not think aesthetics matter much to a lot of people.' Secretly, though, she thought they did. 'But I think when you have a beautiful space it makes you feel beautiful too, and deliciously spoiled. It can be a wonderful escape, a sanctuary from the real world.'

'You're right.' Tian set down his bundle of timber. 'It's not conscious, but it's win-win.'

'More often than not, real life isn't particularly romantic. But every now and again it's wonderful to indulge and feel like we're experiencing life and romance like it is in the movies.' She hugged her sketchpad to her chest. '*That's* what this room is about—it's dream-come-true material. A person who comes to stay here will cherish the memory forever. Gentlemen, we're now in the business of making dreams come true and giving people an experience they'll never forget.'

Their shoulders went back at her words. Zach reached for her sketchpad. 'This—' he slapped the back of his hand to her sketch '—is a piece of cake.'

She bounced on the spot. 'I *cannot* wait to see it once it's finished!'

Janie lugged wood and debris down to the skip, took a turn on the sander and inventoried the deliveries that arrived. She didn't stop. And yet even through the frenetic activity she couldn't shake her continuing and ever-growing awareness of

Zach. Something inside him had lightened and she gave thanks for it.

Not that it made it any easier for her to understand the man. She didn't get him. At all. He acted all judgemental and inflexible one minute and then did something sweet the next. Like setting up a café table for her in the pine grove, and putting locks on the bedroom doors to keep her safe. This morning when the team had arrived he'd told them the third floor was off-limits.

That's not him being heroic. That's him doing his job.

The table wasn't. That was sweet.

'What are you thinking?' he asked on day two of the renovation.

She stood inside the small room behind the bedroom—a storeroom of some kind. There were a couple of them on this floor. This one had shelving on either side. For linen, maybe?

'You're thinking of an en suite bathroom, aren't you?'

She'd refused to turn around when he'd initially spoken because every single time her eyes connected with that big hard body her pulse did stupid things. It was infuriating!

She turned now and found him effortlessly balancing several thick planks of wood across one broad shoulder as if they weighed nothing. Tanned skin shone in the light pouring in at every window and her pulse predictably jostled and surged and her mouth went dry. She snapped back to the storeroom.

'It's big enough, if that's what you're worried about.'

His voice, low and gravelly, had goosebumps lifting on her arms. For the last eight months she'd been indifferent to men and she wanted it to stay that way.

Why now? And why Zach?

'But do we have the time?' she forced out.

'Hold on, let me take this timber through to Darren.'

Why did her stupid hormones have to come out of hibernation *now*? She rubbed a hand over her face. It *had* to be the location. This gorgeous old villa was the epitome of romance, and they were in Greece…on a Greek island. And the sun was shining and the view out of every window stole her breath. The romance of it all had gone to her head.

Zach came back with Tian and together they measured the cupboard and discussed water pipes, waterproofing, timeframes. He moved with a lean-hipped economy that held her spellbound.

So stop looking at him!

Wise advice. But hard to follow. One thing she knew for sure, though—she shouldn't be thinking about sexy times on a Greek island with her hot bodyguard. She shouldn't be contemplating sexy times with anyone! After Sebastian…

Bile burned her throat. This was probably a rebound thing. If she gave into it she might find herself making an even bigger mistake. She couldn't risk it. She couldn't face what that might say about her if she did.

'Janie?'

She came back to earth to find Zach and Tian watching her. She swallowed. 'Sorry, you were saying?'

Zach's eyes searched her face. 'Tian says that he can have it done by the end of the week.'

She straightened. 'Really?'

Tian explained that they'd need to keep things simple—a standard configuration with basic lighting, nothing too fussy when it came to tiles. 'Then we can remove the washbasin in the bedroom.'

All of the bedrooms on the first floor had antiquated washbasins. They were rather sweet, but they didn't scream *luxury resort*.

'That's wonderful. I'll research tiles tonight and we'll talk tomorrow.'

'Okay?' Zach checked when Tian got back to work.

'Very okay.'

'We'll get to work knocking down these shelves, knocking through here into the bedroom, and we'll board up this corridor doorway.' He picked up a sledgehammer and held it out to her. 'Want to do the honours?'

'Yes, please!'

She knocked down shelves, fetched and carried and was general dogsbody. All the while reminding herself that fantasising about Zach was pointless. She wasn't his type. She was a pampered little daddy's girl. Plain Jane.

He said you're not plain.

He was being nice!

He's just being nice, she reminded herself that evening when he brought her out a glass of wine where she sat at the table under the big tree, admiring the sunset. The sea was a wash of pale blues and pinks and so still it made an ache open up inside her.

Lifting his glass of water in a silent toast, he set up a portable barbecue and cooked two steaks to go with the salad he'd tossed and the crusty bread rolls arranged in a basket. They'd agreed to take it in turn about cooking and tonight was his first night. The food looked good, smelled great, and she realised she was ravenous.

He set a plate in front of her before planting himself in the seat opposite. 'It's not fancy, but—'

'I don't need fancy. I need hearty.'

They ate in silence until the worst of their hunger had been slaked. And as long as she didn't let her gaze shift to him too often, safeguarding her pulse from unnecessary jumping and jostling, it was weirdly comfortable.

'Are you disappointed?'

She glanced up. 'About?'

He gestured to the villa.

Oh, that.

'I was initially, but now…' She surveyed the villa's shabby façade, let her eyes roam across the surrounding gardens and then back to the water, which had turned a deeper blue. 'I love this place.'

She frowned. When had that happened? 'Don't you?' she blurted out. 'The villa mightn't be pretty on the outside, but inside it is. And yes, if we're going to do it justice it does lock us into a particular ethos of styling. But what the heck, let's embrace that and go all-in.' She leaned back. 'I find myself…'

Blue eyes flared in the dusk. 'What?'

'Eager to bring the villa back to life.' After his initial lack of enthusiasm, Zach had knuckled down, his dissatisfaction and restlessness melting away. 'Aren't you even a little bit interested in how it's all going to look once we're done?'

He shrugged.

'You know what?' She folded her arms. 'I don't think you hate this job as much as you thought you would.'

Sometimes he was incredibly difficult to read, but now wasn't one of those times. She could practically see the words *Janie has rocks in her head* suspended above him in neon.

She sipped her wine, a luscious red. 'You were humming while you grilled those steaks.'

He scowled. 'Was not.'

'"Sittin' on the Dock of the Bay". Michael Bolton.'

'What the hell...? Otis Redding is the *only* version worth its salt.'

She grinned. That was her favourite version too.

He rolled his shoulders, thrust out his jaw. 'So what if I was?'

'It would indicate a certain level of relaxation and contentment.'

His frown turned inward. Resting her chin on her hand, she allowed herself the momentary pleasure of simply gazing at him while she had the chance.

He stiffened when he realised, his blue eyes spearing to hers. 'What?'

She forced her gaze away. She ought not drink any more wine. It had barriers that should remain steadfast weakening. 'You've been oddly nice to me these last couple of days.'

'Why wouldn't I be nice to you?'

'It's not part of your job description.'

'It's not part of my job description to not be nice to you either. And nice how?' he demanded. 'Because I cooked dinner? It was my turn to cook. Nice because I check all the details of the renovation with you? Well, as you're the boss and the one who needs to approve everything that—'

'You put a café table in the pine grove for me.'

'Just an experiment,' he muttered. 'I wanted to see if you were right. You had coffee there this morning. Did you enjoy it?'

'I did. Why didn't you join me?'

He glanced away. 'Thought you might want to be alone.' He reached for the bottle to top up her wine, but she covered her glass with her hand and shook her head. 'You're surrounded by men on this job, Janie. Seemed important to give you a place to retreat to if you needed it.'

'See? Nice. You didn't have to do that. And you didn't have to buy red wine for dinner either, especially when you don't appear to be drinking it.'

'That's just common courtesy. You're working hard. You need quality downtime.'

And yet that wasn't the impression she had of how he lived his life. He worked hard, but she had a feeling he didn't play hard.

'Can I ask you a question?'

He eyed her warily from behind his glass of water. 'Only if I can ask you something in return.'

Her heart started to pound. What would he ask? What the real Joey Walter was like? Or maybe he'd ask how much plastic surgery her mother had really had done, or which of her stepfathers she most liked now that Mum had married for the fifth time.

'What do you want to ask, Janie?'

'Why you were really so reluctant to take on

this job.' She moistened her lips. 'What did you want to ask?'

He stared at her for two beats and then lifted something that rested on the ground at his feet and placed it on the table. A wrench.

She stiffened. *Her* wrench. 'You've been sneaking into my bedroom.'

'I do a thorough sweep morning and night. Just making sure all is as it should be. *Not* snooping.'

She shouldn't be surprised. And she wasn't really.

'For the last two mornings I've seen this poking out from beneath your pillow. Want to tell me why?'

She hated what it revealed about her. Hitching up her chin, she glared, though he didn't really deserve it. The person who'd sent those awful letters did.

'I figured it wouldn't hurt to have something handy to use as a weapon if the need arose.'

He remained silent. It took an effort of will not to roll her shoulders, fidget…curl up into a tiny ball beneath the table.

Don't be pathetic.

'In case of an intruder… Or something.'

'Or something?'

He wanted her to spell it out?

'You've read those letters. We both know they're probably a hoax, but if they're not that means there's someone out there who wishes to hurt me, who wants to see me suffer. And before you say anything, I know I have a lot of people on my side protecting me and looking out for me, but if this person manages to sneak past everyone then I'm not going down without a fight. So I figure I'm better off with a wrench than without.'

'To give you a chance to knock the assailant out and get away?'

'Exactly.'

'You know the chances of this person getting through are extremely slim.'

'Yes.' She nodded at the wrench. 'But having that helps me sleep better at night.'

'In which case, let's replace the wrench with this.' He handed her a heavy-duty cylindrical torch. 'Army issue. It has a good grip, won't slip, and you can use it as a baton. Once you've knocked the sucker out, you can switch it on to find your way out if it happens to be dark.'

Perfect.

He went to say something else, but both his phone and watch buzzed. He spoke into his watch. 'Sarge?'

'Car just turned into the drive. Headlights off.'

'Roger that. Muting you now.'

She swallowed. 'Do we need to worry?'

'Probably not, but we're going to take precautions anyway. Get behind the tree, Janie.'

She did as he said without argument, taking the torch with her.

'See that branch up there?' He pointed. 'That's where you're going.'

He hoisted her up and one part of her couldn't help but purr at this evidence of his strength and power—those muscles could make a grown woman swoon. Reaching up, he wrapped a warm hand around her ankle as she steadied herself on the branch—standing on it and pressing herself against the trunk.

'I'm not going to let anything happen to you.'

'I trust you.' And oddly enough, she did. Having him near had helped chase away her nightmares too.

'Whatever happens...' They watched the dark shape of a car quietly crunch down the drive and halt. 'Don't move. And don't make a sound.'

Glancing down at him, she mimed zipping her mouth shut. 'Be careful, Zach.'

The car halted, the driver's door opened and someone dressed in dark clothes crept out and tiptoed towards the villa. Her heart picked up speed when Zach left his post beneath her to move out silently and circle behind the man with a stealth that she'd ordinarily admire, except... What if that man was armed?

Damn it! Where the hell with Sarge and the other two operatives? Why weren't they storming the gates and—

Oh, God. Oh, God. Oh, God.

Zach was closing in on the man and...

* * *

With one swift stride, Zach grabbed the intruder from behind, kicked his legs out from beneath him and had him eating dirt as he pulled one arm up in a painful hold and ground an unsympathetic knee into the small of his back.

'Want to explain what you're doing, pal?'

The man wheezed and coughed and swore. 'Jesus! It's me, Zach.'

Zach frowned.

'Cullen. It's Cullen. *My shoulder!*'

Zach eased off a fraction. Damn. The team had done a thorough search on the production crew. Nobody had raised any red flags.

'Jeez, what did you jump me for?' Cullen's voice was muffled by the ground. He wheezed some more. 'Let me up.'

'Not until you explain yourself. Creeping around in the dark isn't making me feel real friendly towards you, Cullen.' He tightened his hold again, making the man groan.

'Okay, okay, I didn't want to blow my cover so soon, but I have to deliver bits of film to you and Janie over the course of the next ten weeks. They're supposed to come from an anonymous source.'

Say what?

'Look, over there.' With an effort that cost him, Cullen nodded towards something on the ground. 'It's an envelope with a cryptic note and a thumb drive. Footage of what's been going on with the other contestants.'

Just to be on the safe side, Zach did a thorough frisk to make sure Cullen wasn't carrying any weapons. Finally letting the man up, he reached for the envelope.

Cullen dusted himself off, eyeing Zach warily. 'What the hell...? Was that necessary?'

Zach shrugged. 'Didn't know it was you. And if we're being brutally honest, I'd have expected better from you. Let me make a suggestion. Don't do that again. We've been working our butts off, we're tired, and I don't take kindly to suspicious intruders creeping around in the dark. They usually mean trouble.'

'And we've all heard tall tales of sabotage on set,' Janie said, ambling up behind them.

What the hell...? He'd told her to stay put!

She ignored Zach to raise an eyebrow at Cullen. 'Why don't you leave the next lot in the letterbox at the top of the drive? Or hand them over in person and have a glass of wine and a chat before heading home again?'

Cullen had the grace to look shamefaced. 'I didn't mean to frighten you.'

The image of that wrench rose in Zach's mind and his hands fisted. Janie lived in enough fear as it was without having to deal with stupid games like this.

A laugh gurgled from her throat. 'As you can

see, we were shaking in our shoes. What on earth possessed you to do something so silly, Cullen? Wine?'

Zach shook his head as she led Cullen down to the table, but she turned and mouthed *laptop* to Zach behind Cullen's back. He nodded.

He returned a few minutes later with Janie's laptop. She'd lit three fat yellow candles and they flickered in the night in the same way the stars flickered on the still water. For the briefest of moments he glimpsed the paradise Janie had spoken about earlier. She was right. There was something about this place.

Setting the laptop in front of her and pointing a warning finger at Cullen when he made as if to leave, he and Janie watched the footage captured on the thumb drive.

Janie stiffened... And then stiffened even more as the footage played. When it finished, she played it again. Antoine, Isobel and several of the other contestants all mocked Janie's charity—and Janie herself. He planted himself on the chair beside hers, fought the urge to reach for her hand and to squeeze it, his insides raging at the unfairness of such a pile on—one deliberately created to make Janie look as bad as possible.

When it had finished playing for the second time, Janie snapped the lid of her laptop shut and glared at Cullen.

He rubbed a hand over his face. 'Look, I don't

make any of the creative decisions or... Or any decisions at all really. I'm told what to film, what questions to ask... And you do know the producers aren't your friends, don't you? All they care about are the ratings and attracting big-name advertisers. And...'

'And?' Janie's voice was hard.

Cullen shrugged. 'Drama sells.'

'That's not drama.' Zach must've said it more grimly than he'd meant to, though, as Janie stared up at him with big, startled eyes. He shrugged. 'It's spite and malice.'

'Don't shoot the messenger.' Cullen held up his hands. 'I already have enough bruises in the service of this so-called drama.' He turned to Janie. 'I'm sorry. I know it's awful. If it's any consolation, I expect everyone will get their turn. You can get your own back then.'

'Sorry to disappoint you, Cullen, but we won't be dissing on anyone.'

Cullen sent them both a weak smile. 'In some ways you could view my drop-off as a public service.'

Zach leant back to stop himself from grabbing Cullen by the collar and shaking the living daylights out of him. 'And you figure that how?'

'We'll be filming your reactions to all of this when the show goes live on Sunday night. At least now you can prepare yourselves.'

Zach was minutely attuned to Janie's every

movement. She chafed her arms as if she were cold and it disturbed the nearby air, sent it brushing against his skin like a breeze. The night was balmy, though, so he knew it wasn't the temperature that chilled her. He'd worked with enough clients who'd felt hunted and vulnerable to know that was how she felt now.

'Have you shown us the worst footage?' he demanded.

'I hope so.' Cullen lifted his hands, let them drop. 'That's the only footage I've been sent.'

After Cullen left, Janie turned to Zach. 'Everyone on the show, the audience at home, they're all going to hate me.'

'Not true. If you were sitting at home watching that, who would you actually be rooting for—Antoine and Isobel?'

'I *never* cheer for the mean boys and girls.'

A whisper of a laugh fluttered through him. 'Janie, I don't believe truer words were ever spoken.' This woman was kindness personified.

She stared at him with wide eyes. Eyes he could fall into. Her scent, all cashmere and violets, made his head swim…the candlelight flickered—

With a squeak, she leapt up, strode around the table and paced for a bit before planting herself in the seat opposite. His heart drummed in his chest. For a moment there he'd been tempted to lean forward, press his lips to hers and—

His gut churned.

She gestured heavenward. 'Why start with me as public enemy number one?'

Because she was the easiest target. He didn't say that out loud.

'Neither Antoine nor Isobel was exactly warm to you on episode one. I guess the director is building on that. If I wanted to maximise the programme's potential drama, I'd be giving Antoine and Isobel enough rope to hang themselves and filming their comeuppance later in the series. It'd make their downfall all the sweeter for the viewer when it comes.'

'Which is ugly in and of itself. And despite what you say, while the audience might detest Antoine and Isobel for being mean, they're probably also going to secretly agree with them. I'm now going to go through the rest of the series with a big black mark against my name.'

'Or because you're the first target and there are another eight episodes to go it gives everyone time to forget what was said during this second week.'

Her laugh lacked mirth. 'You don't believe that for a moment. That's not how these shows work.'

The despair in the depths of those amber eyes chafed at him. Moving, he straddled the chair beside hers, stared out at the water. 'Do you remember what you said earlier about us needing to fully embrace the Greek ethos and styling to do the villa justice?'

'What's that got to do with anything?'

Confusion was better than despair. 'What if you were to wholly embrace the role they're trying to thrust you into?'

Her mouth opened and closed. She cleared her throat. 'You know, that might be worth thinking about.' She drew shapes on the table with her finger. 'Why are you being so Pollyanna all of a sudden?'

Because the haunted expression in her eyes gutted him and he couldn't explain why. Except she'd worked so damn hard for the past couple of days, had been sleeping with a wrench under her pillow, and now he'd witnessed for himself how much she truly loathed being in spotlight. Yet she was still putting herself through all of this for charity. He might not like the charity she'd chosen to support, but he had to admire her dedication.

'Don't know what you're talking about.' He might not be able to change what had happened but he could take her mind off it. 'We were interrupted before I could answer your question.'

'What question?'

'The one about why I didn't want to take this job.'

Cognac eyes immediately lifted to his. Under the glare of her full attention, his nape prickled.

'Water?' she asked when he remained silent.

At his nod, she filled his water glass before filling her wineglass with water too and shifting in her seat to gaze out at the moonlit water. As if aware it might be easier for him to speak if she didn't watch him while he spoke.

Damn it, the woman was thoughtful. But even if she wasn't, after what she'd overheard him say the day they'd met she deserved an honest explanation. Even if it didn't paint him in a particularly edifying light.

'When Sarge, Logan and I left the army we started Sentry.'

She nodded.

'Sarge was always going to be the brains of the outfit while Logan and I were the brawn. Meaning, Sarge would administer and direct operations while Logan and I worked in the field. Obviously, we've a team of people, it's not just the three of us. As we've grown more successful the number of staff we employ has grown too.'

'Makes sense.'

'I've always worked the more dangerous jobs while Logan has worked the ones requiring diplomacy. Each of us playing to our skill set. I'm fit and strong and was one of the army's best hand-to-hand combat fighters in my time there. I can keep someone alive in a jungle or on top of a snowy mountain or in a desert.'

'No way! Really?'

He shrugged. 'Logan is interested in politics, trained in diplomacy and negotiation skills.'

'The three of you make a formidable team.'

'Except Sarge is now talking about retirement and making a succession plan.'

'And you don't want to be stuck behind a desk.'

He really, *really* didn't.

'You *enjoy* dangerous jobs?'

Her incredulity made him smile.

'*Why?*'

'Thwarting danger and bad guys...there's no better feeling." He shrugged again. "I can't say I like the real world all that much.'

The moon lit a golden path across the sea and a small breeze had blown up, making the reflections dance. Pine and salt scented the air.

She was quiet for a long moment. 'So, you don't actually have a home base or anything like that?'

'I've an apartment in London.' Not that he spent much time there.

'But you spend most of your time travelling from assignment to assignment?'

'Yep.'

'What about your birthday and the holidays? Don't you want to celebrate those with family and friends?'

Things inside him tightened. 'I've always been a loner.'

She turned to face him fully. 'There are a lot of good things to be enjoyed in the real world too, Zach.'

Not from where he was sitting, there weren't.

'You didn't look as if you were chafing too

much today or wishing yourself elsewhere. There were times when you looked as if you were enjoying the work.'

He'd expected to hate the work, had expected the associations with his past to plague him. But once he'd found a rhythm all of that had fallen away. He was even looking forward to making that bed she wanted. He scowled, rubbed a hand through his hair. It didn't mean he was going soft or anything.

'Though it's early days and you've been working so hard you probably haven't had time to chafe yet.'

True. Though he couldn't deny there was a certain sense of satisfaction in seeing the bedroom take shape. He hadn't expected that.

'And although this is a *dolly* assignment...' he winced at her words '...I've seen how thorough and vigilant you've been.'

'I'm taking this assignment seriously.'

'I know. I also know what the stats are on the author of those poison pen letters being a crank. But seeing you in action this evening...' She shook her head. 'Cullen had no idea what hit him.'

Which was how he liked it.

'You were amazing, tough guy.'

Her words caught him off-guard. She thought him...

Their gazes caught and clung. Her eyes darkened as they roved across his face, her lips parted, and his heart pounded loud in his ears. She wanted him with the same urgent hunger roaring through him. Heat and elation speared to his groin, the world shrinking to this moment and this woman. Would she taste as golden as she looked—all sunshine and champagne and laughter?

One of her hands lifted as if to reach out and touch his chest, as if to slide up behind his neck to pull it down for a kiss…

The breath jammed in his throat.

Blinking, she snapped away, breaking the spell. Both of them breathed hard.

Before he could say anything, she scrambled to her feet. 'Time for me to head for bed. Goodnight, Zach.'

He stood too.

Janie started for the house. Stuttering to a halt, she turned on her heel, came back and reached for the torch, but her eyes drifted up to his as if they couldn't help it and time stopped.

CHAPTER SIX

AIR SLAMMED OUT of Janie's lungs, leaving her strangely and helplessly immobile. She hadn't meant to come back but she'd wanted the darn torch. Intellectually, she knew she wasn't in danger from the author of those letters, but having a weapon helped her sleep better, helped her feel less pathetic.

Her mistake had been in glancing at Zach… and getting caught up in the turbulent blue fire of his eyes. She'd told herself that she wasn't his type—that he thought her a plain Jane—but that was a lie. She'd known after their first meeting that he hadn't thought her plain.

His stunned *'What the hell are the press thinking?'* had informed her of that. Stupidly, foolishly, it had buoyed her spirits, had fed her vanity. Had made her teasing and flirtatious during their pub lunch.

Pathetic.

She'd told herself the lie because she didn't trust her judgement any more. She'd told herself the lie because of the hunger that stretched through her when she gazed at him. She'd wanted to create a barrier. She had a job to do and things to prove to herself. She didn't want hormones interfering with that.

But all of that fled when she met his gaze, the air between them sparking with heat.

'Janie.'

Her name sounded like a plea on his lips. And when he stared at her like that…

She reached for him and his mouth landed on hers—a sensual assault that had her standing on tiptoe and begging for more. He wrapped her in a heated tenderness that had a moan gathering in the back of her throat. Winding her arms around his neck, she pulled him closer and his groan of approval weakened her knees. She'd have fallen, but his arms held her firmly against him, refusing to let her fall.

He kissed her with a slow and thorough precision as if memorising every line of her lips, as if committing them to memory—unhurried and with a quiet relish that curled her toes…and had a crick starting up in her neck. The man was so tall!

Without breaking the kiss, she pushed him into a chair and straddled his lap. Bracketing his face with her hands, she held him still while she explored his lips with the same slow candour he had hers. The hands at her waist tightened, the fingers digging into her flesh as if it took all his strength to hold still for her.

When she nibbled his bottom lip with her teeth, though, that passion unleashed and he dipped her over his arm, his mouth fierce and possessive, and one hand slid beneath her thigh to pull her hard against the bulge in his jeans and all she could do was hold on as heat and need swamped her and she found herself trying to crawl into his body.

Long moments later his lips lifted from hers and he straightened, breathing hard. She wanted to protest, but the expression in his eyes wasn't horror or regret and it eased the fear that had flared in her chest. Lifting trembling fingers, she touched them to her mouth, unsure if her lips would ever feel the same again.

Drawing her to him, he wrapped her in his arms, her cheek pressed against his shoulder, his chin resting on her head.

'What are you doing?' She was incapable of speaking in anything above a whisper.

Their chests rose and fell in unison. 'Hugging you.'

She closed her eyes. 'Can I ask why?'

She felt his nod and had to swallow.

'Because I don't think my legs will work just yet, which makes me think yours might feel a tad shaky too.'

Understatement much? But…he wanted to stand?

'And not ready to not touch you,' he added.

Okay, cue relief.

'But I think we both need a chance to let oxygen hit our brains again.'

She nestled closer, staring at the water, twinkling with the reflections of a thousand stars. One large hand roved softly across her back in hypnotic arcs.

'I never mindlessly fall into bed with a woman. And Janie, we both know that's where this was heading. I thought you might like a breather before things went that far.'

Wise. And oddly gallant. Smothering a sigh, she straightened, briefly cupped his cheek before forcing herself off his lap.

Piercing eyes searched hers. 'Is this you making a decision?' His gaze never wavered.

She shook her head. 'If you want me to be sensible…well, I can't do that when I'm in your arms. Even if the touch is innocent.'

His nostrils flared as if her words excited him and she had to swing away before she threw sensible to the gutter and devoured him whole. Forcing her legs down to the water's edge, she planted her butt on a large rock, rested her elbows on her knees and her chin in her hands. He sat beside her on the grass. Not too close. 'Want to tell me what you're thinking?'

'I'm trying to remind myself of all the reasons that sleeping with you would be a bad idea.'

'Wanna hit me with them?' He turned his head to meet her gaze. No pressure. No hurt male pride. Beneath his gruffness, Zach had a kind heart.

She let out a slow breath. 'First on my list is that I don't want any distractions. I want to be fully focused on this project.'

'I can understand that.'

And generous. Kind *and* generous.

'But the thing is, whether we sleep together or not, you're already a distraction. I look at you and I want you. I can't help it.'

'I didn't mean to be a complication, Janie.'

She stiffened. 'I'm not *blaming* you. We have… chemistry. It happens sometimes.' Apparently.

'You've felt this before?'

Biting her lip, she shook her head, amazed at her own honesty. Yet it felt right to be honest with him. It felt safe to be honest with him. 'Not like this. This is intense.' All-encompassing. 'You?'

'Not like this,' he agreed.

Her heart pounded. She swallowed and breathed through it.

Remember what's important.

'Zach, I don't feel as if I've achieved much of any note in my life, on my own merit. Take this TV show. I was given it because Joey Walter is my father. But it *is* a chance to show the world what I can do. And I can do it for the betterment of a cause that means a lot to me. That's where I should be focusing my energies.'

His eyes glowed almost midnight in the moon-light.

'And that's why I wish I didn't feel this—' she gestured between them '—thing.'

Reaching for her hand, he pressed a kiss to her knuckles before releasing it again. 'Which is why we shouldn't do this.'

He started to rise.

'And yet…'

He sat again, eyed her warily. 'And yet…?'

'I've been wondering if I shouldn't sleep with you to get you out of my system.'

He stiffened.

'I know. Appalling, right? How cold-blooded does that sound? I've thought a lot of things about myself over the years, but cold-blooded?' She gave an unsteady laugh.

He rubbed a hand over his face. 'Janie, I think you'll find you're hot-blooded.'

'Your turn. Why did you need to stop and think about it? What are your reasons for hesitating?'

Narrowed eyes stared into the darkness. 'I'm supposed to be working. You're a client. My brief here is to keep you safe. I shouldn't let anything get in the way of that.'

She huffed out a laugh. He looked as perturbed as she felt. 'Never had a dalliance with a client before?'

'Nope.'

'We both know that you being here is an over-the-top measure and that my father is being ridiculously overprotective. Your being here is a reassurance to him, nothing more. But it's like calling in a surgeon to put a plaster on a papercut.'

His lips twitched. 'Have you been listening in to my phone calls with Sarge?'

'That said, I know you're taking the job seriously.' Tonight had proven that, to Cullen's regret. 'But your level of expertise isn't necessary.' She chewed on her lip as another thought occurred to her.

'Out with it,' he ordered.

'I don't want you to feel coerced because I'm a paying client.'

He actually grinned at that. 'Not feeling coerced, Janie. There's no boss-employee dynamic here.'

She let out a breath. 'Good.'

'The other thing…'

She raised an eyebrow.

'I don't know where you stand on relationships,' he said with a shrug. 'Do you want one? Is that what you're looking for? Because I don't do relationships. There's no time for them in my line of work. And I wouldn't want you thinking—'

He broke off when she laughed. 'What part of *"I don't like the real world"* do you think I didn't hear? Relationships belong squarely in the real world, Zach.' Leaning down, she caught his eye. 'But in this instance I feel the same.' After Sebastian… She shuddered. 'I'm definitely not looking for anything long-term.'

His gaze lowered to her mouth and her pulse pounded with a reckless surge. Oh, she could—

'If you lean any closer to me, Janie, I'm going to kiss you again.'

She let herself consider tumbling into his arms. She had the Ionian Sea gently lapping at her feet and it was a balmy moonlit night, the air flooded with the scent of jasmine… Talk about an adventure she'd remember forever.

For the first time since Sebastian, it occurred to her that avoiding romantic entanglements didn't mean she had to sacrifice sex. She liked sex. Why deprive herself of it? She'd just need to choose her partners wisely if she didn't want her personal life splashed across the pages of the gossip rags.

Her heart started to pound. Could it be that simple? After Sebastian—

The edges of her vision darkened and a chill chased down her spine. Sebastian had fooled her for two years. *Two years.* She'd thought she'd known him.

Choose a partner wisely?

Ha! How was she supposed to do that when wisdom and discrimination were two traits she clearly currently lacked? And to think she'd thought that she'd had them mastered! It was enough to make a grown woman weep.

Her throat tightened. She had wept. Too much.

But no more.

And no sex for the foreseeable future either. Pulling in a breath, she let it out slowly. She had a goal. It was time to focus on that. When she'd achieved it, maybe then she'd be ready to...consider other things.

'The expression on your face is telling me you've made your decision and that the answer is a firm no.'

Couldn't he try to look a little more disappointed about that?

She shook herself. What the hell? The fact that even *bothered* her told her more eloquently than anything else that keeping her distance from Zach was a wise move.

She made herself smile, but it felt thin and insubstantial. 'You wanted me to be sensible. This is me being sensible. Sleeping with someone isn't the way to make me feel good about myself. Doing the job I came here to do will. *That's* what I need to focus on.'

He didn't say anything. Just nodded.

'And now I'm really going to bed. Goodnight, Zach.'

His 'Goodnight' followed her on the breeze and, no matter how hard she told herself otherwise, it sounded like a promise.

When episode two of *Renovation Revamp* aired, Zach didn't have to jockey for position to sit next to Janie like he'd expected to. Cullen ordered them to sit side by side.

While the team respected him, they *liked* Janie. As they worked, she'd chatter away like one of the woodlarks that visited the pine grove. She'd start silly philosophical discussions like, 'If you were boss of the world what's one fun rule you'd put in place?'

She'd chosen a TV and Internet blackout for Wednesday nights, decreeing that everyone had to join a music group of some sort or play board games. 'How much fun, huh?' she'd demanded.

Everyone had agreed. Except him. He was the strong, silent type, remember?

And then a discussion would start up about what musical instrument you'd play if you had a choice. Or they would go off on a tangent. It was how he knew she could play the guitar.

She knew the names of the team members' families and asked after them, knew who followed what football or basketball team and asked who they were playing at the weekend and what the odds were like. She made them feel like a team. Hell, yesterday he'd checked the scores to see if Darren's and Tian's teams had won. He'd then checked how the team he'd followed in secondary school—Leeds FC—were doing.

He'd snapped his phone shut when he'd realised, his lips twisting. If he wasn't careful, he'd find himself yearning for a white picket fence next!

Ha! Like that was going to happen.

Cullen, however, declared that, for the purposes of filming, he needed Zach and Janie sitting side by side on the sofa, meaning Zach didn't have to fight the other men for the privilege. He'd made sure Darren and Tian knew about the *surprises* this episode had in store, though.

In the upstairs room of the local tavern that Cullen had organised for their private use, Janie, Darren and Tian fidgeted and shifted. When the theme music for *Renovation Revamp* started, Zach's stomach clenched.

The episode was every bit as bad as expected. Between every snippet of renovation they showed of the individual teams, the negative comments directed at Janie and Second Chances mounted up relentlessly. Zach wrapped his hand around Janie's and squeezed, glad when she squeezed back.

'What do you make about all of that, Janie?' Mike asked with his inane grin.

Cullen's cameraman had his camera balanced on his shoulder and pointing at them, but before Janie could speak Tian leaned forward. 'Janie is a very nice woman. She works hard. Why didn't the cameras show her lugging piles of rotten wood down to the skip or sanding the floor?'

Darren leaned into the camera's view too. 'Tian's right. Seriously uneven footage and—'

'Team, team...' Janie started to laugh, but a light

had fired to life in her eyes and Zach couldn't work out if that was a good thing or not. He guessed they were about to find out. No denying, though, that it made her look alive, as if someone had just plugged her into the electricity mains.

Which then had him thinking about that fire-cracker of a kiss. His skin stretched tight.

Don't think about the kiss.

It should never have happened.

'As you can see—' Janie gestured '—I have the best team. These guys have been great. They've worked their tails off all week, but we've had a lot of fun too. Now, Mike, you asked for my thoughts… I'm pleased with the score the judges gave our bedroom renovation. Team Puerto Rico did an amazing job and deserve to be top of the ladder at the moment, but equal second is a nice position to be in.'

'And what about all of the negative comments directed at you and your charity, Janie? That has to hurt.'

'In the interests of full disclosure—' she pressed her hands together and stared at the camera, her chin high '—someone leaked part of that footage to me earlier in the week. I think I was expected to retaliate with some mean girl comments of my own in an attempt to smack down my detractors.'

She was magnificent.

'But I'm not going to do that. Nobody here has yet heard why I'm such an advocate for Second

Chances or the good work the charity does. That footage was filmed prior to being on location, so I know it'll appear in an upcoming episode. Second Chances is an easy target because it's not a *pretty* charity, and to be honest all of that bad sentiment simply feels like a cheap attempt to create fake drama.'

'Hear, hear,' Zach murmured.

Darren and Tian both nodded.

'What I would like to say, though, Mike, is that I'm dedicated enough to Second Chances that I'll be donating my appearance fee to the charity. I sincerely hope the other contestants are doing the same for their chosen charities. Perhaps they can let us know next week?'

'Cut!' Cullen called.

When the episode ended Zach turned to her. 'That was pitch-perfect.'

Her eyes lightened at his words, but then her gaze snagged on his mouth and her nostrils flared. 'Thanks.'

They shot to their feet at the same time, moved apart. What the hell was wrong with him? She'd said she didn't want anything to develop between them. He had to respect that and stop the mooning and ogling. Pining like some pathetic teenager. His hands clenched. Unlike his father, he *could* control his baser instincts.

The rest of the team gathered around Janie to offer their support and Zach moved across to the window to scan the street outside with a professional eye. While waiting for the wholly unprofessional ache in his groin to subside.

This was what happened when he wasn't on some high-powered assignment. It left him adrift and all at sea with nowhere to direct his pent-up energy or—

You know exactly where you want to direct that energy.

Displacement, that was all this was.

He had to rid himself of any thought of making love with Janie. Tian was right. She was a nice woman. She worked hard. He didn't want to make her job here harder than it already was. Despite his body's protestations, the decision she'd made was the right one.

In his world, women like Janie had always been off-limits. The Janies of the world always eventually wanted more. He didn't have *more* to give. He didn't stay in one place long because he didn't want emotional attachments, especially not of the romantic kind. As far as he was concerned, love was emotional suicide. Only a fool or masochist would put themselves through it, and he was neither.

His childhood had been defined by fear. And helplessness. Never knowing what would trigger his father's violence—his sheer defencelessness against it when it did erupt. The helpless fury that he could do nothing to protect his mother.

An ache stretched through his chest. Love and commitment had led his mother to heartbreak and misery. He wasn't making the same mistake. It had taken him a long time to feel secure, to find his place in the world. He would never hand anyone the power to make him feel that scared and helpless again.

They made the trip back to the villa in silence.

He glanced from the road to her and back again. 'You stressed about what Antoine, Isobel and the others said about you?'

Golden eyes sparked with surprise. 'Hell, no! I couldn't give two hoots what Antoine and the rest of them think. I don't know them. They don't mean anything to me. They're not my family or friends. Water off a duck's back.'

'Not entirely sure I believe you,' he said, but that only made her laugh.

'Look at who my parents are. I've been surrounded by exaggeration and drama and hyperbole my entire life. People saying mean things about them, and me, all because…'

'They're famous. And in an attempt to grab a little of the spotlight for themselves,' he finished for her.

She tapped a hand to her chest. '*I'm* the party-pooper who's always the voice of reason. Whenever Mum or Dad fly into a tizz over a bad review and it's all "This is the end of the world, I'm so untalented, my life is over" drama, I'm the person who makes the tea and talks them down.'

Yeah, he could see that.

She snorted. 'Antoine is an amateur when it comes to insults, while Isobel insinuates a lot but there's no substance behind it.'

He frowned. Something didn't add up. 'You were gutted when you first saw that footage.'

'Gutted for Second Chances, not because someone said something mean about *me*. I'm here to lift Second Chances' profile, not damage it. But I couldn't change what they planned to air tonight so I had to suck it up.'

He pulled the van to a halt in its spot behind the villa. There was something he wasn't getting. And he planned to find out what it was, but first he had an online meeting scheduled with Sarge.

When the meeting was done, he grabbed a can of soda and started down to the table under the big tree where Janie sat with a glass of wine. Halting, he swung back, searched the kitchen cupboards for snacks—olives, cheese and crackers—and took them down to her.

At her raised eyebrow, he shrugged. 'Dinner seems a long time ago.' They'd eaten early due to the show. She'd eaten next to nothing. 'Thought you might be hungry.'

'I'm good.' She sipped her wine. 'You tuck in, though.'

Something was wrong. And if it wasn't Antoine and Isobel...

Popping an olive into his mouth, he chewed and swallowed before chasing it down with a mouthful of soda. 'You must be pleased. The judges loved what you did with the bedroom.'

Her head swung around, her eyes widening. *'Seriously?'* She gaped at him.

Whoa!

'They loved what you and the team did. Tian's en suite was pitch-perfect, the treatment of the stone wall inspired, and the bed you built a masterpiece of craftsmanship, whereas I—'

She what?

Shooting to her feet, she marched down to the edge of the lawn and stared out to sea. He scratched a hand through his hair. What the hell was he missing? 'Janie?'

'I let you all down. *I'm* the weak link.'

He was on his feet and in front of her in a millisecond. 'What the hell are you talking about?' He had to step down to the pebbly beach to face her and it put them nearly at the same height. He tried to ignore the shape of her mouth. 'What part of second place didn't you hear? You—'

'And what part of *I played it safe and didn't take risks* didn't you hear?' She jabbed a finger at his chest. *'That's* what one of the judges said.'

'She also said your use of colour was incomparable and that the overall harmony was superb.

And she acknowledged you needed to make decisions between balance and budget. The other judge said it was a bedroom he'd love to sleep in. Why are you focusing on that one quibble?'

Her glare didn't lessen.

'Janie, I didn't know you were going to go full drama queen on me. There weren't any notes in your file to warn me about this.'

'I'm not...*a drama queen*!'

'Well, where on earth is that voice of reason you boasted about earlier? Where's the water off a duck's back? Because I hate to tell you this, but you're doing the whole over-the-top exaggerated thing you just accused your parents of doing whenever they receive a bad review.'

Her mouth worked but not a single sound emerged. Her eyes sparked and her chin thrust out. But as he watched, it all slowly bled out of her. Her shoulders drooped and with a funny little hiccup she stumbled back to the table and fell down into the nearest seat—his. He hesitated for a moment before heading around to her seat and switching their drinks. She looked as if she needed something stronger than wine.

'They say pride comes before a fall, don't they?' Her voice was shaky, and it pierced through the usual protective armour around his heart, making it ache. 'I feel as if there's some Greek chorus above my head pointing a finger and laughing itself silly at me right now.'

He didn't know what to say. He should've brought chocolate rather than cheese and crackers. He sliced off a piece of cheese, stuck it on a cracker and handed it across to her. She demolished it, a martial light in her eye. He made her another one, and then another.

'It's just that's what I always thought I was good at—not getting swept up in the nonsense, seeing the bigger picture and maintaining my equilibrium, keeping perspective... Cutting through all the noise to see to the truth. My dad is great at singing, my mother is great at acting, and I'm good at...'

'Wading through all the hype. Seeing the facts.'

She stared at her hands. 'All my life I've seen my parents swing between the highs and the lows that comes from living their lives in the spotlight. Similarly, they've always been totally over the top in their praise of me. That kind of upbringing can go to your head.'

She'd had such a different childhood from his. And he was glad of it. Didn't mean it hadn't had its challenges, though.

'I was lucky enough to have had a very wise nanny. Nanny Earp, who taught me to look beyond all of the noise and nonsense and to see it for what it was. She taught me to question everything, because everyone has an agenda—reviewers, theatre critics, producers, fans...one's peers. And while some people are genuine, others are pushing their own agendas. She taught me to recognise hyperbole and exaggeration and to understand how they distort reality. She taught me to come to my own conclusions about what was true and false, and to not simply believe either the good or bad press.'

Which explained why she hadn't thrown a temper tantrum when she'd overheard him grumbling on the phone to Logan that first day.

'Nanny Earp sounds like quite a woman. Where is she now?'

'She retired to a little house in Suffolk that my parents bought for her. I see her regularly. She's unofficial family.'

He sliced more cheese and handed it across. She ate as if on autopilot, but he was glad. She needed to keep her strength up.

'So what happened, Janie? What made you overreact to one little comment a judge made tonight?'

Her lips twisted. She gulped wine. 'Sebastian happened.'

CHAPTER SEVEN

'SEBASTIAN. YOUR EX-BOYFRIEND.'

Of course Sebastian would be in whatever file they'd compiled on her.

'Then while we're speaking of agendas—' Zach eyed her steadily '—let me push mine for a moment.'

'You want to know if I think Sebastian could've written those letters.'

His eyes gave the tiniest of flickers—a minute narrowing and release—as if he knew it was an awful question, but it was his job to keep her safe and he'd do it regardless. She fought an entirely inappropriate desire to reach across and lay a hand against his cheek.

No touching!

'Well, they did arrive after we broke up. And the breakup wasn't amicable.'

'Go on.'

'And he'd take great delight if I were publicly humiliated or if my business failed. But those letters...' She shook her head. 'I just can't see it.'

Though she'd been spectacularly wrong about Sebastian in other ways. 'Never say never, I suppose.'

'But you'd be surprised if he was the culprit?'

'Really surprised. They just don't sound like him. And while he might like to do me a bad turn, he wouldn't risk his own neck to do it.'

'The man sounds like a toad.'

'Total toad.'

Something in his face gentled. 'What did he do, Janie? How did such a toad manage to shake your confidence so badly?'

She reached for another slice of cheese and slammed it onto a cracker.

'Did he cheat on you?'

'Not that I know of. Though I suspect that would've been easier to deal with. Some men are incapable of fidelity—the grass is always greener, the thrill of the chase and whatever other nonsense they tell themselves. It has nothing to do with the attractiveness or worth of their girlfriend. And before you say anything, I know some women are like that too. But while that would've hurt me, I'd have managed to maintain a degree of objectivity. I'd have kicked his sorry butt to the kerb and moved on, older and wiser.'

She crunched her cheese and cracker with a savage satisfaction. Zach ate an olive and remained silent—not hurrying her, just waiting.

'All my life I've had people befriend me to try and get close to my parents. Sometimes they're after money, sometimes they want an introduction to a recording studio executive or a film producer. Sometimes they want the kudos of moving in what they see as exalted circles.'

'According to your file, you don't move in exalted circles.'

'I don't usually, but most people wouldn't believe that. For me a great night out is getting together with Beck and Lena, ordering in pizza, drinking cocktails and watching a romcom.'

Zach nodded. 'Few things can beat watching *Match of the Day* with Sarge and Logan, cold beer in hand.'

'And see? If you stopped hurdy-gurdying all over the world, you'd get to do more of that.'

That amazing mouth stretched into a rare smile. 'Hurdy-gurdying?'

Her heart pitter-pattered, her pulse did a samba and her chest billowed like a parachute filled with air. She stuck her nose in the air, hoping none of that showed. Because *nothing* was going to happen between them. She *was* going to be sensible. 'You know what I mean.'

She couldn't hide the breathlessness of her voice, though, and it had his gaze lowering to her mouth.

Swallowing, he pushed the dish of olives away to seize his soda and ease back in his chair. 'Back to Sebastian.'

She dragged her gaze from the powerful lines

of his shoulders to fix it on the villa behind him. The villa she'd fallen in love with. Taking two steadying breaths, she prayed the breathlessness would ease. She and Zach might be attracted to each other, but there were good reasons for not following through on it.

She sipped her wine. 'Right, so… I learned pretty early on to work out if people had an ulterior motive when it came to befriending me. I've had a lot of practice at it over the years and I've learned to read the signs, recognise the red flags.'

'But it sucks.'

She shrugged. 'It is what it is. And some people would consider it a small price to pay for the privileged life I lead.' He opened his mouth as if to argue, but she shook her head. 'Everyone has challenges in their lives, Zach—things they need to overcome. In the general scheme of things, mine are small.'

'Janie—'

'Anyway—Sebastian,' she cut in. 'We met at a nightclub. I hardly ever go to those places, but it was Beck's birthday and it's what she wanted to do.'

'Had you been drinking?'

She had to laugh at his less than subtle suggestion that she'd need to be drunk to go out with Sebastian.

'We were both being the sober friend who'd get the others home safely. He was fun, easy to talk to, and when he suggested we meet for coffee some time I didn't see any harm in it.'

Blue eyes flashed in the semi-dark. 'He was too smooth by half.'

'That's the thing, though. He wasn't.' At least he hadn't acted like it. 'He was a bit bumbling and awkward, which made him oddly endearing.' She bit her lip. He'd played her so well. 'He didn't pretend not to know who I was, but he didn't ask a single question about my parents.'

'But it was all a façade?'

She ran a finger around the rim of her wineglass. 'As it turns out. But at the time nothing he did or said made me suspicious. And I'm not the kind of person who's forever falling in and out of love.'

'Me either.'

That didn't surprise her.

'I led him a merry dance, and yet he kept bumbling along and not giving up.'

'Until he wore you down.'

'Until I trusted him. And then I let him into my inner circle.'

'Beck and Lena?'

'They liked him too.'

'Your parents?'

'Mum liked him. Dad will never like any of my boyfriends.'

Those lips curved into another toe-curling smile.

'Nobody will ever be good enough for Daddy's little girl?'

'I could sing the chorus to the song,' she agreed, which made him laugh, and had the heavy things inside her lifting. 'We were together for two years before I found out Seb was only dating me to get access to Joey Walter and the music industry movers and shakers among my father's cohort.' She stared at her hands. 'I didn't even know he wanted to be a singer.'

He'd sing in the shower, and she'd tell him she loved the sound of his voice, and he'd beam at her whenever she said it. That had been it.

'I'm sorry.'

'I didn't know until he threw a massive temper tantrum about my father refusing to back him and urging me to intervene on his behalf. I hadn't even known he'd raised the topic with my father or requested a meeting. That's when I knew.' She paused, collected herself. 'I gave him a chance to prove me wrong. I told him I never interfered in any music or business decisions my father made, and that I wasn't about to start now.'

'What happened?'

'He told me I owed him. That he'd spent the last two years making me happy on the unspoken proviso he'd be rewarded with Joey Walter as his mentor. I asked him why he hadn't told me he wanted a career in the industry, and he said because he knew it would've made me suspicious. And you know what he said? He said, *"I will marry you and make you happy if you make this happen for me."'* She shook her head. 'Talk about delusional.'

'Weren't you the slightest bit tempted?'

'What the hell, Zach?' She reared back. 'No way! Why would you even ask such a thing?'

One shoulder lifted in a seemingly casual shrug, but she sensed the tension behind it. 'I knew someone once who made compromises like that.'

Her stomach churned. Someone he'd loved? When he didn't add anything, didn't explain, she didn't dig. The expression on his face forbade it.

'I showed Sebastian the door.' Blowing out a breath, she stared up into the branches of the tree. 'It wasn't a pretty scene.'

'Did he try to hurt you? *Physically?*' The words barked out of him like bullets.

'Nothing like that. Just said a lot of vile things about me being a bad girlfriend, boring, and a crap interior designer. And that I'd only got where I was because of my parents.'

A scowl darkened his face. 'And you're letting his opinion now cloud your judgement and have you doubting yourself?'

'Don't be daft. I couldn't give two hoots what Sebastian thinks or doesn't think about me. Not any more. What do you take me for—some delicate little petal?'

He blinked.

'What's thrown me is that for two years I had no idea of Sebastian's true colours. *For two years.* I believed in him; I trusted him. I... I thought he loved me. But all that time he was using me. I was nothing more than a pawn. And I never sensed it. I didn't see it until the bitter end.'

All of the cheese she'd eaten churned in her stomach. 'I thought I could read people. I thought it was my superpower. From the age of twelve I've done my best to keep my parents from their wildest flights of either despair or euphoria by reminding them that a particular reviewer might have been less than complimentary because of an incident that happened three years ago, and that another singer or actor might have been super complimentary because they're hoping for a good soundbite for an upcoming album or film they have coming out.'

Pity she hadn't been able to do that for herself.

'For most of my life I've reminded them that they're super talented and super successful, and not to pay too much attention to the hype either way, to stand firm in their own worth.'

'Keeping them grounded.'

And trying to keep herself grounded too.

'But if that really was my superpower I'd have seen Sebastian for what he was. Two years, Zach. He fooled me for *two years*! And if I was so wrong about Sebastian, what else have I been wrong about?' That was what really chipped away at her self-confidence—what else was she wrong about? How could she ever trust herself again?

'Janie, what he did to you was unforgivable.'

'Can't you see this isn't about him? It's about me.' She slapped a hand to her chest. 'I thought I could read people, but Sebastian proved me wrong.' And it had shattered her world and left her reeling. She'd been ready to build a life with a man who'd lied and tricked her, and been ready to keep up that lie forever. Had there ever been a poorer lack of judgement?

Of course there has been, the sensible part of her snapped.

She wasn't the only person who'd been taken in by a liar and a cheat, but...

She'd been so totally and incomprehensibly wrong about Sebastian, and now she couldn't trust in anything. Perspective had flown out of the window. The fear of being that wrong again—about anything—crippled her.

'You made one mistake in one person. We all make mistakes. You need to stop beating yourself up about it.'

She huffed out a laugh. 'Beck and Lena tell me the same thing. It's why they urged me to do the show. They thought it'd boost my confidence.'

'I like these friends of yours.'

'They tell me to stop beating myself up and move on, chalk it up to experience. But the fact is I don't feel as if I am beating myself up.'

Those blue eyes pierced into hers and she wanted to blow the candles out and drench them in darkness in the hope that it would lessen the intensity.

'How do you feel?'

Though maybe it *wasn't* intensity and she was *mistaken* and simply imagining it.

'That I can never trust my judgement again.'

He sucked in a breath that sounded loud against the water lapping on the shore and the crickets cheeping in the garden.

'I always thought I was a pretty good interior designer. I studied hard, my teachers were complimentary, and I work hard now. I love transforming a room—or a house or apartment—and making it look wonderful in a way that delights its owner and makes them happy.' Achieving that brightened both her and her clients' worlds.

'I know I gained some of my early jobs due to who I am. It's inevitable and I have no way to combat that. But I thought, now I was established, that I was being sought on my own merits, that it was my own reputation that had started to precede me, rather than my parents'.' She met those peculiarly intense eyes again. 'But what if all of that *is* wishful thinking?' How would she bear it if she discovered she'd been wrong about all of that too?

Zach reached across the table, seized her hands in his and squeezed them hard. 'You're a brilliant interior designer, Janie. What you did with the bedroom over this last week has been breath-taking.'

She wanted to believe him, but...

'And the judges recognised that. We came second, Janie. We're only a whisker behind Team Puerto Rico.' His grip tightened. 'You want some advice?'

'I only want good advice.' And these days she wasn't sure how to tell the difference between good advice and bad. So what was the point?

He shook her hands as if reading that thought in her face. 'My advice is the best.'

She rolled her eyes. 'Of course it is.'

'Focus on the entirety of what the judges say—don't take one tiny piece of it and worry at it with the kind of focus your parents have always done and blow it out of proportion. It's probably your default setting because that's what you saw growing up, but Nanny Earp taught you better than that.'

Zach had the most ridiculous desire to hold his breath as a range of emotions raced across Janie's face. She pulled her hands free from his and it left him oddly bereft. He swiped his palms down the sides of his cargo shorts, tried to rub the feel of her away. It didn't work.

She ran her hands over her face. Eventually she pulled them away and nodded. 'You're right. Nanny Earp did teach me better and I should be doing her proud rather than making a mockery of all that she taught me.'

This woman put too much pressure on herself.

She dragged in a breath that made her entire frame shudder. 'Right, back to basics.'

'Back to basics,' he echoed. What were the basics?

'She said I had to be my own compass. Don't fixate on just the one line that stung in a review, or half a paragraph in the paper, or phrase in an entire conversation. Take it as a whole. Only then could I make an informed judgement.'

He opened his mouth, but she held up a finger. Silhouetted by the light of the moon and with the Ionian Sea as her backdrop, she looked like a Greek goddess. Need rose through him, hard and fast. His mouth went dry. His groin went tight. He wanted this woman with a raw hunger he'd not experienced since he was a teenager. It took everything he had to remain in his seat and not to act on it.

She'd said no. He *would* respect that.

'She'd tell me to take into account who made the comments and why they might be making them.'

Ignoring the throb and burn of his body, he nodded. 'Sometimes what's being said is more a reflection of the speaker than who or what they're talking about.'

'Nanny Earp had a saying—it's a quote from

Robert J Hanlon. *"Never attribute to malice that which is adequately explained by stupidity."'*

Nanny Earp's philosophy had his full approval.

That cute nose wrinkled. 'Of course, that's not the kind of motto that'd work in your line of work.'

Which was a shame. Maybe—

He blinked, straightened, shook himself.

What the hell...?

He refused to mourn the lack of stupid people in his life. The life he'd chosen was the *right* life. He didn't belong in Janie's world. He didn't *want* to belong in Janie's world.

Pulling in a breath, he folded his arms. 'So what did that judge say *in its entirety*? And why might she have said it?' Seizing her laptop, he found the replay of tonight's episode and fast-forwarded to the judges' comments, hit play. When it finished, he spread his hands. 'Well?'

She sucked her bottom lip into her mouth and it was all he could do not to groan. 'I have a good grasp of colour and proportion,' she started slowly. 'And our bedroom complemented its surroundings.'

'What else?' he urged when she paused. He pointed to the laptop. 'They said you handled the budget really well.'

A finger tapped against her lips. 'That was a deliberate decision. I'm trying to save the bulk of the budget for the big reception room and the outside space.'

The colour had returned to her cheeks and he let out a careful breath. 'Do you wish you'd blown the budget to avoid the *playing it safe* comment?'

'The criticism would've then inevitably been that I'd spent too much money,' she said slowly. She dragged in a breath. 'And that judge is known for her innovation, her playfulness with form— that's her *thing*. That's how she'll be judging everything on the show.' She slumped as if some great tension had drained out of her. 'Every team received at least one positive comment and one "room for improvement" comment.'

She sagged in her seat, glancing across at him. 'And as far as criticisms went, ours was pretty mild. Oh, God! I don't know if I should laugh or cry, but you're right. I panicked and blew all of that out of proportion. Just call me Joey Walter or Colleen Clements.'

'Okay, Joey or Colleen or whatever your name is, you should definitely laugh.'

Her shaky laugh threatened to split him in two.

'Not that I'm not good with crying damsels,' he found himself babbling. *Shut up, idiot.* 'But you're no damsel, Janie. You're smart and capable and you're talented.' And damn Sebastian to hell for making her doubt herself. If he ever got his hands on that slimeball—

'And good with panicking drama queens ready to throw themselves off cliffs too. Thanks for talking me down, Zach.'

His heart beat hard and he willed it to slow. 'Nanny Earp did most of the heavy lifting.'

She stared at him for a long moment, folded her arms. 'You seem strangely reluctant to take any credit. Keeping someone alive in the jungle or on top of a snowy mountain isn't the only way to be a hero, Zach.'

She thought him a hero? The expression in her eyes caught him in a web of longing. He should look away, but he didn't want to.

'If you hadn't pulled me out of that negative spiral...'

Her lips shone in the candlelight. 'I've seen both of my parents descend into the pit of despair. It's awful. It takes so much energy for them to climb out again. If that had happened to me here, I'd have started second-guessing myself, constantly changing my mind, stressing everyone on the team out and—'

She broke off. 'It would've been awful. I'd have ruined everything. But you helped me gain perspective before that could happen.'

She made him feel like a superhero.

'I know you're here first and foremost as my bodyguard, but tonight you've been the voice of reason and I can't tell you how much it has helped. Or what it's meant to me.'

She moistened her lips. Hunger roared through him.

'I know that being here is making you chafe.'

Except he wasn't chafing. And that ought to worry him. Being stuck here, grounded, should have him tearing his hair out. Yet when he stared into that golden-eyed gaze, he couldn't be bothered with any of it—couldn't be bothered working out what it meant either.

'I really am grateful, Zach, thank you.'

He wanted to seize her in his arms and kiss her until—

He cut the image dead. He didn't force himself on women. He *wasn't* his father.

'You ought to go to bed, Janie.'

She swallowed. Her nostrils flared as if she could read the battle raging through him. Temptation crept across her face, making her eyes glow.

'Bad idea,' he ground out. 'You don't need or want distractions, remember? I'm here to help, not hinder. I promised.'

He could say something ugly to create distance between them, something that would send her marching stiff-backed to the house. Something like him not being sure she could keep her emotions from becoming embroiled if they did embark on a steamy affair—suggesting he knew her better than she knew herself like some patronising prat. Utter tosh, but it'd do the job.

But he couldn't do it. Janie had enough ugliness in her life. He wouldn't add to it. 'Goodnight, Janie.'

With a nod, she stood and made her way back to the house.

It took all his strength not to call her back.

They started working on the dining room the following day.

The team trailed after Janie as she moved into the large room that opened to the left of the wide entrance hall. 'This is our dining room. There's a paved patio out of the side doors there for alfresco dining, and the same big windows at the front looking down to the sea as the other reception room. It could be a beautiful room.'

The team started inspecting walls and floors, door and window frames, and the state of the ceiling. Zach planted his hands on his hips when they were done. 'Repair-wise, there's not much to do in here.' Like all the other rooms, the door and window frames needed replacing and new shutters fitted. 'Hit us with your vision for the room.'

'Right, I want this room to be full of colour to reflect the sun and the sea. This is a room to live in, a place to enjoy good food and good company. I want it to be stimulating without being overwhelming.'

She listened to the suggestions the team made and made adjustments as needed. She was, quite frankly, amazing. She might've said she wouldn't have the scope to experiment here like she would at a beach resort, but from what he could tell she wasn't letting that hold her back.

'I don't want it to look too formal or uniform so I'll be using an assortment of tables that were already here. They'll need some mending and painting, but we might need a couple of extras. Do we buy or build them?'

'Build them,' they all said at once.

'I don't want to skive off, but at some stage I need to do some shopping. I'd like to showcase some local wares to thank the town for being so helpful.'

The villagers had been delighted to have them here filming. Nothing had been too much trouble.

He couldn't let Janie venture out alone, but… 'How about we put in a full day today and then see how we're travelling tomorrow?' He glanced at Darren and Tian. 'We could start earlier and finish earlier.' It'd give Janie time to browse the shops before they closed.

Darren glanced up as if realising where Zach was going with this. 'There's a market in the village tomorrow afternoon.'

Janie's eyes lit up. It made something inside him lift too. He tried to stay cool, look unfazed. 'And there's that little mezze place across from the waterfront if anyone is up for dinner afterwards. Who's in?'

Everyone sounded their agreement—even Cullen's production crew.

* * *

Seven days later they trooped back into that up-stairs tavern room to watch the next episode of the show—all surreptitiously girded for battle—but things went as smooth as butter for Team Greece. Janie's styling and vision were unanimously celebrated, and the local arts and crafts she'd seamlessly incorporated into the room—beautifully handcrafted bowls, a spectacular wall hanging and embroidered tablecloths—admired. At the end of the episode Team Greece found themselves in equal first place with Team Whitsunday, while Team French Polynesia trailed one point behind.

Janie's smile, the way her eyes sparkled, her *delight,* knocked the breath from Zach's lungs, made his heart race. Retreating outside, he did two laps around the tavern before leaning against a tree on the other side of the road to keep watch.

He needed to get a grip. Janie wasn't the first woman he'd ever wanted and she wouldn't be the last. He dragged a hand down his face. Maybe Sarge was right. Maybe he needed to make the time to focus on things other than work once in a blue moon.

And that didn't mean he was going soft! It was just… He couldn't recall craving any woman with the intensity he craved Janie.

Clenching his jaw, he dragged in a breath. It'd be easier to resist her if he didn't like her so much, but he refused to get hung up on her. He wasn't becoming emotionally engaged with any woman. He didn't *do* emotional vulnerability. He wasn't repeating his mother's mistakes. He'd lived that nightmare once. Never again. He'd worked too hard to make himself strong and unassailable to throw it away now.

Seven days later they once again assembled in the tavern. They hadn't received any further *secret* footage, and he'd started to breathe easier.

The first half of the show went smoothly—for Team Greece at least. Team French Polynesia had a shocker and he could see Isobel gritting her teeth. The judges were again complimentary about Janie's styling of the family bathroom that had been this week's challenge. They'd praised her use of local tiles while her colour scheme again drew admiration.

'I'm afraid, though, Janie—' Mike, the host, gave a smarmy smile '—that it has come to our attention that you've broken the rules.'

She leaned forward, staring intently at the TV. 'Broken them how?'

Zach leaned forward to whisper, 'Cullen is filming,' so she'd know to be on her guard. The brief touch of her hand on his knee acknowledged that she'd heard him, and had the blood surging in his veins.

'You worked the team longer than the prescribed eight hours.'

She straightened. 'I did not.'

Footage of the team at the village market last Tuesday afternoon played on screen.

She gaped. 'That wasn't work! We were socialising, having fun. We went out for dinner afterwards.'

Darren and Tian muttered their agreement. It made no difference. They'd apparently *'discussed plans for the villa'* and that counted as work. They were deducted five points and Darren and Tian banned from working on Monday. They dropped from first place to third.

'We have someone here who says you often don't play by the rules, Janie. Your ex-boyfriend, Sebastian Thomas.'

What the...?

He curled his hand around hers. This now felt personal. Did someone within the network have an axe to grind? Were they out to get Janie, or Joey Walter via Janie? Was this the same person who'd written those threatening letters?

Fury built as Janie gripped his hand tighter and tighter as Sebastian—the scheming, lying, snake in the grass—droned on about how Janie's good girl, clean-cut image mattered more to her than the people in her life. He claimed that she'd used and abused him, and had then tossed him aside like a dirty rag.

'And we're now going to a live feed in Greece... What do you say to that, Janie?' Mike threw at her.

Zach stabbed a finger at the camera. 'I'm saying you're scraping the bottom of the barrel if you're now bringing people's exes onto the show. And if you think that smarmy toad is a defender of truth you're dumber than you look, Mike.'

'Oho, and I see you're still playing knight in shining armour, Zach. It looks good on you!'

'If Janie cared about her image,' Tian growled, 'like this Sebastian claims, she'd be supporting one of those pretty, feel-good charities. But she's not. He lies.'

Go, Tian.

'It appears that you're surrounded by knights, Janie. You don't have anything to say in your own defence?'

Janie straightened. 'I'm torn between saying *No comment*, which is the classy thing to do, and what I've always said in the past…'

She paused. Zach glanced at her.

Folding her arms, she lifted her chin. 'Except have you noticed it's always women who are told to be classy and remain silent—less said soonest mended and all that don't rock the boat nonsense?' Her eyes narrowed, the gold in them flashing. 'Ladies, we need to stop putting up with that garbage. The fact of the matter is Sebastian used me—pretended to be in love with me to gain access to my father.'

On screen, Sebastian's jaw dropped, his shock palpable.

Go, Janie.

'When Joey Walter refused be Sebastian's mentor or endorse an album for him, and I refused to intervene on his behalf… Well, let's just say the truth came out. As you'd expect, and as any sensible woman would've done, I kicked his sorry butt to the kerb.'

Both the building team and production crew cheered.

'Was your father's assessment of Sebastian's talent correct, or was it coloured by your opinion?'

'Look, Mike, Sebastian has a YouTube channel. If you're so inclined, you can go and listen and decide for yourself whether he has talent, or if Joey Walter was right when he said that Sebastian has a monopoly on mediocrity.'

'What's your opinion on the matter?'

'That's my father's area of expertise, not mine.' She pushed her shoulders back. 'What I can tell you is that Sebastian is a liar and a cheat and I'll be happy if I never hear his voice again.'

CHAPTER EIGHT

JANIE FELL DOWN into one of the armchairs they'd placed in the kitchen and stared across the room. Had she just made a fool of herself on national television, and in the process blackened the reputation of the charity she was supposed to be supporting?

She closed her eyes and dragged in a breath, but Sebastian's face rose in her mind—his smirk, his lies—and she found her hands clenching so hard her entire body shook, her mind going over and over what she'd said in retaliation, making her wince again and again. *Oh, God, she shouldn't have—*

'Come on.'

She snapped to when a big warm hand curved around hers and pulled her to her feet. The warmth and understanding reflected in Zach's incredible blue eyes had a lump forming it her throat. And it had her swallowing against the want that heated her veins, despite the agitation roiling through her.

He led her outside and down towards the table

beneath the big tree. He urged her to sit, and she watched as he unpacked the bag he'd had slung over one shoulder. But all the while she couldn't stop Sebastian's words from going around in her head, couldn't stop thinking what a terrible ambassador she was for Second Chances.

He produced a bottle of dessert wine. 'Name five things you can see.'

She blinked.

'Go on, humour me.'

Him. She saw him.

Don't say that.

Swallowing, she forced her gaze to their surroundings. 'I can see the silhouette of the big tree against the sky. And the sky is a shade lighter than navy because the moon is so big tonight there's a lot of light. We almost don't need the candles.'

He lit them anyway and produced a container of baklava.

'I see a bottle of Sauterne and a dish of baklava and...' She stared at the water and a slow breath left her. 'And the shoreline where those little waves are rolling up onto the rocks looks edged in silver.'

'And in your usual fashion you've excelled. The tree, the sky, the moon, candles, Sauterne, baklava and the shoreline. That's seven.'

She blinked. 'How did you do that?' Her agitation, while not gone, had receded enough for her to draw oxygen into her lungs.

'It's an old army technique for battling anxiety.' He sat. 'What can you hear?'

'The crickets, the water splashing, the call of a night bird I don't know the name of...your voice.' She let out what she hoped was a quiet breath. 'You have a good voice, Zach, deep and low, unrushed. You could be a radio DJ if you wanted.' She frowned, things inside her clenching. 'Do you sing?'

'I can hold a tune well enough, but I'm no singer. The life your father leads...' He shook his head. 'It's not for me.'

Of course it wasn't. The tight things unclenched again.

He set a piece of baklava in front of her, poured a generous slug of wine in one glass and a splash in another. 'You were brilliant tonight.'

She grimaced. 'No, I—'

'I'd like to propose a toast.' He lifted his glass.

Frowning, she lifted her glass too.

'Tonight you stood up for women who've spent too much of their lives being belittled and bullied by men. I don't think I've ever been prouder to be associated with anyone than I was tonight.'

Her jaw dropped.

'To you, Janie, for leading by example and refusing to let bad behaviour and slander go unchallenged.' He touched his glass to hers, but when she didn't raise it to her lips he frowned. 'Do you regret what you said?'

She had been, but...

'I don't regret sticking up for myself and setting the record straight.' She wrinkled her nose. 'I shouldn't have said that bit about him having a monopoly on mediocrity.'

'Best smackdown I've heard in ages.'

'It was mean, and I don't like being mean.'

'You were put on the spot. You had next to no time to compose yourself, let alone prepare something pretty to say. You showed grace under fire and you should be proud of yourself. Also, Janie, Sebastian should never have gone on national television and said the things he did. So he can't complain if he doesn't like the outcome. He had it coming.'

When put like that...

He touched his glass to hers again, raised an eyebrow.

She took a sip. 'Thanks, Zach.' He'd talked her down off a ledge *again*.

'I don't think you recognise the value of what you did tonight.'

That had her shaking her head. 'I'm not the only woman to ever call a man out.'

'There can't be too many voices.' His fingers drummed against the table. 'I happen to feel strongly about this.'

She could see that.

'I've had first-hand experience of what happens

when a woman is too frightened to take a stand and stick up for herself.'

Her gaze lifted and her heart stopped. The expression in his eyes...

It took all her strength to remain in her seat rather than move around the table to put her arms around him. She had to swallow before she could speak. 'Who?'

Shadowed eyes met hers. His nostrils flared. 'My mother.'

The breath punched from her body. She wanted to hit something.

Reaching across, he removed the wineglass from her grasp. 'Cheap glass. Wouldn't take much to break. And the last thing you need is stitches in your hand when we have a room to renovate next week.'

Even now he was looking after her. But who'd ever looked after him? She moved around the table to sit beside him, peered up into his face. She didn't take his hand, although she wanted to.

'Your father?'

A tic started up in the side of his jaw. 'My father was a violent man. He abused my mother with words *and* his fists.'

She pressed a hand to her mouth to hold back a gasp...and a far from ladylike curse. But as Zach had just toasted her for what some would consider unladylike behaviour, he probably wouldn't mind her cursing.

'I'm sorry.' She swallowed carefully, forced her hands not to clench. 'Did he hit you too?'

He didn't answer. He didn't have to. She saw it in his eyes. Everything inside her drew as tight as a bow. Puzzle pieces fell into place.

'I worked in construction for a number of years when I was younger.'

'He made you leave school to work for him,' she said slowly. *What a weasel.*

His laugh was bitter. 'I shot up when I was fourteen, filled out. That's when he realised he had a use for me and I started working for him part-time. At sixteen, he hauled me out of school altogether.' His eyes narrowed, his mouth settling in a cruel line. 'But working in construction means you develop muscles, and I'd had enough of him by then and started fighting back with hard fists of my own.'

Everything she had ached for him. He shouldn't have had to suffer that. No one should.

'At sixteen I could physically defend myself, give as good as I got, but I could still be emotionally manipulated.'

Cold dread spread through the pit of her stomach.

'When I wasn't home, he started giving my mother the beatings he wanted to give to me.'

She covered her face with her hands.

'Hey.' He pulled her hands away. 'It was a long time ago.'

'That stuff stays with you forever.' She dragged in an unsteady breath. 'Tell me she left him.'

He dropped her hands. Reaching for his baklava, he bit into it as if needing the sweetness. Her heart sank, but she did the same with hers. The flaky pastry, the honey and nuts followed by a sip of the sweet wine helped to ground her in the present.

'How did you end up in the army?'

'When I was eighteen I was done—I left home. I refused to be manipulated by my father any more. I wanted my mother to leave him, promised her I'd look after her. I started working for someone else, found a house to rent, but she refused to leave.'

A lump lodged in her throat. 'Why?'

'She said she loved him.'

He looked so suddenly lost that she wrapped a hand around one huge bicep and rested her head against his shoulder, her eyes burning.

'Here's something they don't tell you about abusive men, Janie. They can be Jekyll and Hyde.'

'Meaning?'

'Meaning they can be charming and charismatic, until the switch is flicked.'

She couldn't imagine staying with someone who hurt her... Even if she loved them.

'Her mother was timid, as were all my aunts. My grandfather died when I was small, but from all accounts he was a domineering man. She had no one to show her how to stick up for herself. Or to tell her she deserved better.'

Her hand found his and she squeezed it tight.

'That's why what you did tonight, and what you said, matters.' He pressed her hand between both of his own. 'You showed other women—and men too—anyone who watched the show, an example of how to stand up for themselves, how to call out bad behaviour, and that it's okay not to settle for less.'

He'd made her see this evening's events in such a different light.

They sipped their wine in silence. 'Do you see your mother any more?'

He shook his head. 'When I was eighteen and still trying to get her to leave my father, I turned up one day to find her black and blue. I lost my temper and when my father got home we came to blows. The police were called.'

Her stomach churned.

'My mother refused to press charges against him. He threatened to have me charged with assault unless I stayed away and didn't see either him or my mother again. My mother said that's what she wanted. She begged me to stay away.'

Her heart caught. 'Oh, Zach, I'm so sorry.'

'One of the policemen took me aside and talked to me about the cycle of abuse. He told me that until my mother made the decision herself, there was nothing I could do. He also told me it wasn't uncommon for the son of a violent man to become violent himself, and that I was displaying the early signs.'

'What the hell?'

He laid a hand on her arm. 'He was right. I'd have never hit a woman, but another man…' He shrugged. 'He advised me to get a change of scenery, gave me a brochure about joining the army.'

'And you took his advice.'

'I didn't know what else to do. And the army kept me busy, gave me a purpose, gave me a place to channel my anger while giving me something to work towards. I ring my mother every year on her birthday and at Christmas and leave a message, but so far she's never returned my calls. I've an aunt I talk to a few times a year. She tells me how the family is getting on—keeps me up to date with my mother's phone number and where she's living…' He trailed off with a shrug.

'Wow, Zach. I…'

He smiled as if he knew all the things she wanted to say. 'The army was good to me. I got a degree, developed skills, made lifelong friends.'

'So why did you leave?'

'Sarge, Logan and I decided we wanted to be our own bosses, and that's worked out great.'

'You're amazing,' she breathed. 'If anyone here should be proud of themselves it's you.'

His brows shot up.

'After everything you've been through, you're

a good man. You didn't go off the rails. Instead, you became a living, breathing crusader for those weaker than you. You're...a superhero.'

'Not true.' He rolled his shoulders. 'I just do what I can. Do what's needed.'

'I'm sorry I pulled you away from working on important things. No wonder you hate Second Chances. Your father is a criminal who should be locked up and the key thrown away.'

She'd bet that black and white world view of his had kept him alive more often than not, and kept alive the people he protected.

'Do you want to hear a real confession?'

The expression in his eyes held her spellbound. She nodded.

'I'm not the least bit sorry to be here. I'm *glad* to be here.'

She couldn't help herself then. She reached up and kissed him.

Janie's lips on his threatened Zach's every semblance of control, whipping him into a frenzy of need and heat. His tongue tangled with hers, his fingers diving into her hair to curl around her scalp and pull her closer. He wanted to bury himself in her, take everything she offered. He wanted that oblivion with a greed so all-consuming he had to pull back and drag air into starved lungs.

He stared down at her glazed eyes and swollen lips. She—

What the hell?

Putting her away from him, he shot to his feet and backed up two steps, the taste of panic bitter on his tongue. 'I *won't* take advantage of you.'

She blinked. 'I beg your pardon?'

He backed up another step. 'You said you didn't want distractions.' No matter how hard he tried, his heart refused to slow. 'You said you didn't want this to happen.' He *would* heed her wishes.

'But—'

'I've had to use all of my resources over the past few weeks to stop myself from kissing you, touching you.' He jabbed a finger skywards. 'And I'm not asking for applause or a pat on the back, but I'm *not* going to ruin all of that hard work now by taking advantage of you when you're feeling fragile and grateful and—'

'Hold on a minute—'

'I am not my father!'

Silence followed his bellowed words and it had his nape prickling.

Behind the soft caramel of her eyes, he sensed her mind spinning and whirling. Very slowly, she stood too. 'You're *nothing* like your father, Zach.'

Because he held himself on a tight rein, kept himself in check and refused to be ruled by his emotions.

'Your father was all about control and coercion. You've been nothing but protective and kind.'

Because he worked hard at it. 'But if I let things between us go any further…'

'That still wouldn't make you like your father.'

He *wanted* to believe that.

'You've helped me feel empowered. You listened to me and let me help to come up with our cover story. When you found the wrench you gave me a better weapon instead of patronising me and laughing at me.'

'You're smart and proactive—that doesn't deserve to be laughed at.'

'See? Definitely not like your father.'

Her words lightened something inside him.

'And I think you're forgetting something. *I* kissed *you*.'

Yeah, but he'd kissed her back.

'You've done nothing wrong. If someone should be blasting themselves it should be me.'

He shook his head. 'It's been an emotional evening—'

'And maybe I would be if I regretted it, but I don't.'

For a moment everything—the wind, the waves, the twinkling of the stars—froze. What was she saying?

'I like kissing you, Zach. I want to do a whole lot more of it.'

But… 'You said…'

'I know what I said.' Her eyes never dropped from his. 'Back then it seemed the right thing to do. The sensible thing. Back then I couldn't decide if falling into bed with you would be a mistake that'd distract my focus. Or an inspired move that would send my creativity soaring and...'

The pulse at the base of his throat pounded. 'And?'

'Be the best adventure of my life.'

The best... Something frozen at the centre of him started to thaw. He bent until they were eye to eye, needing to make sure he'd heard her correctly. 'You want to kiss me?'

'Madly.'

'You want to do a whole lot more than kiss me?'

'I want to make love with you.'

His breath quickened. Violets and cashmere flooded his senses.

She lifted her chin. 'Interested?'

'Yes.' The word left him without hesitation. She shouldn't be the only one here putting herself on the line. 'I want you so much I'm shaking with it. That's the problem. I've wanted you too much. It shouldn't have been so damn hard to remember what *you* wanted.'

She reached up and touched his face. 'You haven't done anything to make me feel pressured, Zach. You're not that kind of man.'

He could no sooner stop from kissing her than he could stop the tide. She tasted like honey and wine, summer and warm breezes. He fell down onto a chair and pulled her onto his lap and drank her in. Winding her arms around his neck, she melted against him. Nothing in his life had ever felt more real. Nothing had ever felt this good.

Slipping a hand beneath her blouse to touch warm skin, he lost himself in the feel of her. Janie arched into his touch when he cupped her breast, her nipple beading to a flatteringly hard nub as he brushed his thumb across it. The little sounds she made in the back of her throat incited him to push the blouse up, pull her bra to one side and draw the nipple into the hot warmth of his mouth.

Her cry pierced the air and in a flash the summer breeze became a thunderstorm. Fingers dug into his arms, the short nails raking and urging him on, not that he needed urging. He'd gone rock-hard and needy. She tasted like sin and salvation and he was starving for both.

Pulling back a fraction, he dragged air into starving lungs. They stared at each other, both breathing hard, eyes glittering.

Lifting herself higher on his lap, she caught his face in her hands. 'Neither of us is the other's true north. I'm not looking for anyone to be my compass, but you make me feel…'

He raised an eyebrow.

'Better.' The breath left her on a whoosh. 'I was feeling like crap and you've made me feel better, calmer, more at ease with myself…happier.' She shook her head as if it was a miracle. 'You've made me like myself more.'

A lump lodged in his throat.

'You're a great big gorgeous, squishy stress ball, Zach Cartwright.'

Her words surprised a bark of laughter from him. She had him hot and bothered *and laughing*. The combination was shockingly seductive.

'I know you said you didn't want to be a distraction, but I'm thinking distraction is exactly what I need.' She bit her lip, looking oddly vulnerable, and it occurred to him how much she hid that side of herself from the rest of the world. To see it, to be allowed to see it, left him moved, humbled. Honoured.

'And just so you know, I'm well aware that what happens on a Greek island stays on a Greek island.'

A hot summer fling with this extraordinary woman…? His pulse spiked. A better man might pull back, but he wasn't a better man.

'I take exception to squishy.'

She glanced down—cheeky, flirtatious, those lovely lips curving up. 'I see your point.'

'But we're not doing this outdoors.' He lifted her off his lap. 'We've cameras monitoring the perimeter of the property, but…'

Her gaze lifted to the first-floor balcony. 'There's a romantic bedroom up there that I think we've earned the right to.'

Without another word, they moved back to the house. On the landing at the top of the stairs Janie turned and swallowed. 'I feel I ought to go and put on something seductive and—'

He swooped down and claimed her mouth in a hungry kiss, backing her up against the nearest wall, running his hands down the sides of her body, making her tremble and moan. He kissed her like a warrior intent on subduing a rival—not giving her time to think or react, bombarding her instead with sensation as he made short work of the buttons on her blouse and dropped it to their feet. Her jeans followed.

'Mission accomplished,' he rasped, lifting his head, his mouth tingling from the intensity of their kisses, his bottom lip burning from the way she'd sunk her teeth into it in mindless passion, before laving it with her tongue.

She wore nothing now but a pair of simple cotton knickers. They were a shocking red against the pale honey of her skin and stars burst behind his eyelids.

'*That's* what I call seductive.'

She pushed a finger into his chest, breathing hard. 'Where did you learn to kiss like that?'

He crowded her against the wall again. 'Is that a complaint?' He didn't wait for an answer, but rubbed his chest against hers. Her breath hitched. 'Undo the buttons on my shirt, Janie.'

Dazed eyes lifted at his command, excitement

glittering in their depths. 'Are you trying to scare me, tough guy, with the bad boy act?'

She wasn't scared and they both knew it.

Lowering his head, he gently bit her earlobe. 'You've been boss for over three weeks now and I think it's time someone else took the reins so you don't have to make any decisions or do any of the thinking. I'm in charge now.'

Her fingers fumbled on his buttons and he smiled against her neck as he pressed a series of kisses there. 'Push the shirt off my shoulders, sweetheart.'

She did. As if his words hypnotised her.

Insinuating a thigh between her legs, he pressed against the sensitive core of her. Her head dropped back and her breathing grew ragged.

'You want a stress release? Then I plan to give you one. You won't be thinking, you won't be making plans, the future doesn't exist here. All you'll be doing is focusing on the now and sensation.' He eased his thigh away and then pressed it back again, and her eyes glazed and she caught her bottom lip between her teeth.

'When I'm done, Janie, you're going to be limp and satisfied. *Very* satisfied.'

A tremor shook through her.

'So I suggest you hold on tight.' He lifted her into his arms. Golden eyes gazed into his. 'If that's okay with you,' he murmured.

'It's very okay,' she whispered, running her fingers through his hair, and he realised how much it had grown since he'd been here, and how much he liked the sensation of her fingers against his scalp.

The moon glittered through the glass of the French windows. He laid her on the bed and stared. Bathed in moonlight, she looked like some Greek goddess—all silver and gold and achingly beautiful. But when he lowered himself down beside her she was all warm womanly flesh and he took his time exploring every inch of it with lazy hands and tongue and mouth.

She arched into his touch, her hands tugging at him mindlessly, her moans and sighs urging him on, begging him for release. He built her to a fever-pitch of excitement—never had his own need been so...secondary. He made her come with his mouth, and then he built her to a fever-pitch level again and only then did he kick off his cargo pants, roll on a condom and sink into her silken flesh.

Her eyes flew open and found his in the moonlight. Her lips parted as if on a revelation, and then she smiled and he found himself lost in it as they moved together, setting a rhythm. With each stroke, though, he fell deeper, felt more, moved beyond anything he'd ever experienced.

Gritting his teeth, he tried to focus on nothing but increasing her pleasure... But her hands on his back... The way her legs wrapped around his waist... The sharp bite of her teeth at his shoulder. It dragged him under until all he could think, feel and want was Janie.

Her body bowed, her muscles tightened and she cried out—exhilarated, exuberant. Moving with a will beyond his own, he too flung over the edge. Pleasure spiralling through him, a hoarse cry dragged from the depths of him. The intensity, the pleasure, lasted...spread out...gentled.

As he floated back down, he rolled onto his back and gathered her against him, feeling remade.

He woke early. Unlike the bedrooms on the second floor beneath the eaves, this room faced east and sunshine flooded the room, gilding it in a warm glow—a magical Greek island benediction.

Janie lay on her stomach, arms flung out, her eyelashes making dark half-moons against the creaminess of her cheeks. Last night had been—

He had no words for it. Maybe it was the result of all the banked heat that had built between them. Maybe it was the magic of the island or the hothouse atmosphere of the show. Or maybe it was simply the woman herself. Janie might consider herself ordinary, but she was wrong.

He let her sleep. It was Monday. Darren and Tian were grounded. It'd do her good to rest, to catch up on some sleep. To take some time off.

Dragging on a pair of shorts and T-shirt, he headed downstairs. He'd bet she'd enjoy breakfast on that balcony with its amazing view. Poached eggs, sourdough toast and peaches. He started gathering breakfast things when his phone buzzed.

Logan. Pressing it to his ear, he said, 'What's up?'

'Found out Sarge went to school with Joey Walter.'

The air whistled between his teeth. 'No way. Old friends?'

'Looks like it.'

'And on the health front?'

'His cholesterol is up and he's showing signs of being prediabetic.'

'He keeps himself fit.'

'But he likes a beer and a burger a little too much, apparently. It can all be reversed by a healthier eating plan.'

'Sarge has to go on a diet?'

'Yep.'

Hell, no wonder he'd been in such a foul mood.

'Neither of our lives will be worth living if you let him know that we know this, Zach.'

'Roger that. And thanks, mate.'

No sooner had he rung off than Sarge called. 'Found out something interesting. Janie's ex has started dating again and you'll never guess who it is.'

His lip curled. 'Whoever it is has seriously bad taste.'

'Isobel Jamison.'

'Of Team French Polynesia fame? You have to be kidding.' At his side his hand clenched and unclenched. 'Are the threatening letters linked?'

'Sabotage rather than a personal threat? Distinct possibility. Isobel clearly has an axe to grind where Janie's concerned, but whether that's because of her relationship with Sebastian or because Janie's design skills are streets ahead of anyone else's on the show is anyone's guess.'

Zach nodded. 'Those skills have surprised a few people.' Because Janie really was exceptionally talented. 'But if Isobel already had that intel from Sebastian, maybe the letters were an attempt to persuade Janie to pull out of the show.' His finger tapped against the phone. 'Do we know why she might want to win the show so badly that she'd go to those lengths?'

'I've Jo and Tully on the case.'

Good call. They were both exceptional agents.

'There are rumours that Isobel's character in the drama series could be written out. If that happens, she'll be out of work.'

He mulled that over. 'She needs to lift her profile to either keep her current job or find another.'

'That's the theory. We're going to keep digging, see what we can find, but it's looking more and more likely that Janie isn't in any physical danger.'

A hard knot inside him loosened. They'd never

really thought she was. But it was good to have their suspicions confirmed.

'Zach, I know I came down hard on you, son, but it was important to me that we gave this job everything. I want to thank you. I know it's not the kind of job you enjoy. And...' he hesitated '...I shouldn't have snapped your head off when you asked if Joey Walter was blackmailing me. The thing is, I know Joey from back in the old days.'

So Logan was right.

'You serious?' He feigned surprise.

'He's a good guy.'

'Well, if we're doing confessions... This job hasn't been as bad as I thought it'd be.'

Sarge chuckled. 'I don't believe that for a moment.'

'I haven't enjoyed the fake drama and the cameras, but the building...'

Sarge was quiet for a moment. 'I thought you'd hate it because of your father.'

'Me too. But I don't.' He rolled his shoulders. 'Just thought you'd like to know. Didn't want you worrying about it. Now, next question,' he forged on. 'Janie's like her dad—she's a nice woman. Last night's episode shook her up.'

'What are you thinking?'

'That a day away from this place might do her good. Thought we could go play tourist in Corfu town.'

In the background he heard Sarge tapping away

on his keyboard. 'It's busy, lots of people—you'll blend into the crowd— Yeah, I don't see the harm. Me and the crew will keep an eye on the villa.'

They rang off, and Zach made breakfast. When he walked into the bedroom, Janie was stirring. Opening her eyes, she blinked up at him and her slow smile smacked into him like a big warm hug.

He tried to keep his voice even. 'I have a suggestion.'

'Whatever it is, I say yes.'

CHAPTER NINE

JANIE'S PULSE GALLOPED at the sight of Zach wearing nothing but a pair of soft cotton sleep shorts and white T-shirt, holding a tray of something that smelled delicious and smiling as if all was right with the world. She wanted to hug herself.

'But first, madam might enjoy breakfast on the balcony.'

With a grin, he nudged through the curtains at the French windows. Ooh! The way the cotton of his shorts hugged the muscles of his thighs and backside...

Deep breaths, Janie. Deep breaths.

Last night had been amazing, but it was probably a good idea—necessary—to let the poor man get some sustenance before dragging him back to bed.

Actually, last night had been better than amazing. It had...

Thought stopped as images played through her mind. She doubted words could capture precisely how amazing the previous evening had been.

Zach poked his head through the French windows. 'Coming?'

She might feel fabulous—reinvigorated and restored—but she was also stark naked and she wasn't sitting out there wearing nothing but—

Then she saw her silk wrap sitting at the bottom of the bed, and Zach's thoughtfulness had her stomach softening.

'Yes,' she said, unable to hide her breathlessness—or eagerness. Actually, with Zach, she didn't feel as if she had to hide anything.

When he disappeared back behind the curtain, she scrambled out of bed and pulled the wrap around her and nipped into the bathroom to roughly finger brush her hair and splash cool water onto hot cheeks, before padding out to the balcony.

The view should've stolen her breath—a green lawn sloping down to water that was millpond smooth, the only sound the morning chorus of birds and the lapping of water. But when blue eyes speared to her as she hovered in the doorway, darkening in appreciation, all she saw was him. For one heart-stopping moment she thought he might leap to his feet, haul her into his arms and kiss her.

Instead, he poured her a mug of coffee and gestured for her to take a seat, his hand not quite steady.

Perching on a chair, she lifted her mug and inhaled the steam. 'This looks wonderful.' It was as if he'd not only heard her words during the renovation of the bedroom but had memorised them, intent on making her vision of romance a reality.

Something in his shoulders eased. 'Eat, Janie.'

She took a piece of toast, grabbed a peach, glanced out at the view and then back at him. He raised an eyebrow. She bit into a corner of her toast.

'Something on your mind?'

Come on, you stood up for all of womankind yesterday. Don't let yourself down now.

'Last night was…'

Both of those eyebrows rose.

'It was wonderful, Zach.'

His shoulders, his spine, the muscles of his forearms all relaxed as if her words had melted him like wax. 'Couldn't agree more.'

'Really?'

He'd started to cut into his egg on toast, but halted. 'You doubt it?'

Her cheeks heated. 'I sort of got swept away and…'

'And?'

'Well, I'd hate for it to have been one-sided and— Well, I just want you to have enjoyed it as much as I did,' she finished in a rush.

He leaned towards her. 'Last night was extraordinary. All of it.' He placed a hand on his heart. 'I'm looking forward to doing it again if that's what you want too.'

'Again and again,' she said, a grin rising through her.

They ate their breakfast, casting surreptitious

glances at one another, appreciative and admiring…hungry and lusty.

When they'd finished Zach cleared his throat. 'I thought it might be fun to go into Corfu town today.'

She blinked.

'We deserve a day off. We've been working hard and I suspect you're going to say we need to get to work on the reception room. But we've done a lot in there in our downtime during the last few weeks and even taking into account that we won't have Darren and Tian today we're ahead of schedule. Also, who knows what other inspiration we'll find if we get out and about a bit and learn more about the island?'

She opened her mouth, but he held up a hand. 'Neither one of us has been to Corfu before. I'm curious to see more, aren't you? And,' he added before she could speak, 'if you remember, you already said yes to my suggestion.'

She started to laugh. He wanted to spend the day with her? It was all she could do not to hug herself. Perhaps it was irresponsible, but they were ahead of schedule. And to have a whole day with Zach away from here? Talk about dream-come-true stuff and making memories.

'I think that's an excellent idea.'

Something in his face lightened. 'You do?'

'Can I suggest an amendment to the plan,

though? The shower in the en suite is big enough for two…'

Before she was even aware of it, he was on his feet and she was in his arms and they were naked and warm water was pouring down over them in a delicious stream, but hot water wasn't the only thing that steamed up the bathroom mirror.

The town of Corfu was larger than Janie had expected—they'd barely seen any of it on the drive from the airport. They wound through quaintly cobbled alleyways with colourful shopfronts painted a variety of pastel pinks, greens, blues and yellows, the strip of bright blue sky above an invigorating contrast. She bought gifts for Beck and Lena—colourful bead necklaces and olive oil soaps—and a Greek fisherman's cap for Zach that he promptly placed on his head. He surprised her with a gift of a pretty dish she'd admired.

'What's your favourite thing to eat?' she asked as they walked along the waterfront with its row of tantalising restaurants.

'Seafood. We didn't have it much when I was growing up.'

Because his father hadn't liked it? She didn't ask. She didn't want thoughts of his father marring their day.

'And you?'

'Pizza.' She smiled. 'For much the same reason.'

They chose a restaurant with a forecourt right

on the water, a large awning providing shade, the splash of pink bougainvillea cascading over the restaurant's whitewashed façade utter perfection. They ate seafood pizza and shared a carafe of local white wine with bold notes of summer fruits and spring flowers. After lunch he captured her hand in his and followed a set of directions on his phone.

'There's something I think you'll like.'

Winding along several streets, they eventually turned and squeezed down an alley no wider than her arm span, merging into a beautiful courtyard. A fountain stood at its centre, the path surrounding it bordered with cypress trees. Beneath the trees sat wooden benches. The surrounding buildings were all of honeyed brick. Water cascaded from the mouth of a dolphin on one wall. Resting against the other walls were troughs and hanging baskets overflowing with pansies, petunias, geraniums. Moving to the fountain, she turned on the spot. 'It's magic.'

'Apparently it's a closely guarded local secret.'

Trust him to have found it then.

With his hands on her shoulders, Zach urged her down to one of the benches. 'What's your favourite gelato flavour?'

'Strawberry.'

He disappeared down an alley, returning soon after with two gelatos. They ate them soaking up the atmosphere and throwing around ideas about how to create something like this on a smaller scale back at the villa.

Afterwards, she took him to a museum of Roman artefacts where an ancient village had been recreated. While he marvelled at the craftsmanship of the old masons, she marvelled at him.

They bought lovely things from a deli—bread, feta and a slab of hard yellow local cheese, spiced olives, cured meats, locally made ginger beer— and took them home to have a picnic supper at the table beneath the big tree. Which they did, sitting side by side as the sun went down.

Janie rested her chin in her hand and drank it all in. 'What an absolutely magical day.'

His gaze roved over her face and he sent her one of his rare smiles. 'Exactly what the doctor ordered.'

'For me or you?'

'Both. We've been working our tails off. It was good to have some R&R.'

She blinked.

'What?'

'That's not something you'd have said a month ago. A month ago R&R was the last thing on your mind.'

Two lines appeared on his brow. He rolled his shoulders and her stomach clenched. Had her words made him think she was trying to change him? Had they made him think that the lovemaking and the fun they'd had today meant more to her than it should?

She swallowed. Had it?

Don't be ridiculous.

She knew this fling would end as soon as their Greek adventure was over. And she was totally okay with that. She flipped her hair over her shoulders. As she'd told Zach, she wasn't looking for anything long-term. She wasn't ready to have her heart broken again. Doing a great job on the villa was her first priority, but where was the harm in having some fun along the way?

Reaching for an olive, she popped it in her mouth, gave a careful shrug. 'I'm glad it hasn't been as awful as you expected. For all I know you could be an amazing actor, but—'

'I hope I'm an excellent actor when the situation requires it, but you're right.' His frown deepened but it was in consternation rather than annoyance. 'I expected to be bored, constantly chafing…restless, but I haven't been. I've enjoyed the work and watching the villa transform. And I like our team. Darren and Tian have been great to work with.'

His words made her pulse race, but she didn't know why. 'Ditto to all of that.'

'And you—' he pointed a finger at her '—are an interesting woman and good company. This job has proved anything but boring.'

She knew she must be grinning stupidly, but she couldn't help it. Didn't want to help it.

'I'm sad we've only a few more weeks left.' Well, they still had a whole month and a half, but the time seemed suddenly precious. 'I suggest we make the most of it before we have to return to our not so ordinary worlds. Starting right now.'

'Excellent plan.'

They gathered up the debris of their meal, left the dishes in the sink and, taking Zach's hand, Janie led him upstairs and had her wicked way with him. She wanted to learn the shape of his body, the sound of his breath quickening when she did something he liked, the way his body tightened and jerked.

'Janie, you're killing me,' he finally groaned. 'If you—'

He didn't get any further as she sheathed him with a condom and lowered herself down onto him. His fingers dug into the flesh of her hips, the air whistling between his teeth. She loved watching him like this—unguarded—a compelling combination of fierce and vulnerable. She could stare at him all night long and not grow tired of it.

Heavy-lidded eyes opened, spearing into hers, and a lazy thumb lowered to circle the most sensitive part of her, making her gasp. Before she knew it, she was moving with a new urgency that shut out everything else. Their cries of release echoed around the room when they climaxed. It should be illegal to feel this good.

Afterwards he pulled her against him and she rested her head against his chest. When their breathing had returned to normal she pressed a kiss to the firm, warm skin beneath her. 'Let's play a game of hypotheticals.'

'After what you just did to me, we can do whatever you want.'

She grinned and kissed him again. He tasted of salt and something darker, like cloves or rum. It was a taste she could become addicted to. Resting her chin on her hand, she stared up at him. 'I think you've fallen into the habit of only seeing yourself according to your role with Sentry.'

He raised an eyebrow.

'I think you're so much more than a hotshot bodyguard, Mr I-Don't-Like-the-Real-World Cartwright. For one thing you're seriously skilled with your hands.' She laughed when he ran his hands down her body, all teasing temptation. 'You're a natural leader, but a team member too— smart enough to take advice and let everyone play to their strengths. And you're a good friend.'

The teasing light in his eyes disappeared. Her mouth went dry. 'I know that I've been a job to you, but I also feel like we've become friends.'

Janie's words speared into Zach with a sting he didn't understand.

'And I hope that when this is all over, we can remain friends,' she continued. 'Maybe catch up for the odd meal or drink when you're in London.' She traced patterns on his abdomen. 'I know a lot of people, Zach, but I don't have many friends. I like to keep the ones I do have.'

Had all of this meant more to Janie than he wanted it to?

Yet a part of him yearned for what she offered. To catch up with Janie once in a blue moon for a drink or a bite to eat, to make sure she was safe and happy... Where was the harm in that?

'So that's hypothetical number one: if we're friends, can we catch up in the real world every now and again when this adventure is over?' Before he could answer she rolled onto her tummy to stare fully into his face. 'Because here's the thing, Zach.'

He sat up against the pillows. What thing? She wasn't going to say she'd started to fall for him or—

'Eventually you will have to retire from your high intensity fieldwork.'

What the hell...?

She ignored his glare. 'One day you'll be eighty and while you'll probably be an insanely fit eighty-year-old, you won't have the lung capacity you once did, and you'll probably need a knee replacement from that old injury you have and—'

'How do you know I had a knee injury?'

She shrugged. 'Lucky guess. Sometimes when

you've been crouching down for a while, you stand up and flex it and give it a rub.'

He did?

'So…' she continued. 'While retirement might not be imminent, I think we can agree that eventually it's inevitable.'

Her words made him feel like an idiot. Because *of course* it was inevitable. That was all Sarge and Logan had wanted him to admit and come to terms with. Instead of agreeing with them he'd bitten their heads off.

He moistened his lips. 'So what's the hypothetical question there?'

'Well, when you're no longer playing superhero, what do you want to do if you don't want to be stuck behind a desk?'

He frowned.

She nudged him with a soft laugh. 'We're playing a game. You don't have to be so serious about it.'

Except eventually he was going to have to be serious about it, wasn't he? And while she might not know it, she'd made him see that being prepared and having a plan would make the transition easier.

On second thoughts, scrap that. She knew *exactly* what she was doing.

'Okay, play genie and tell me what you see in your crystal ball.'

Sitting up against the pillows too, she feigned

staring into a crystal ball. 'Ooh, Mr Cartwright, your future is full of promise and adventure. I see travel to far-flung places—snorkelling in Australia's Great Barrier Reef, jet skiing in Jamaica, skiing in Banff... I see prawns on barbecues and cocktails on the beach and hot chocolate in ski lodges. Oh, and wait, there's something else... poker tournaments in Vegas as well as—'

'I can't spend my entire life on holiday, Genie Janie.'

She gave an offended sniff, but her eyes danced. 'You wouldn't be doing those holidays one after the other like some playboy gadabout.'

He tried to rein in a smile. 'No?'

'Of course not. They'd be your reward for taking a rundown French château—or Greek villa—and bringing it back to life and turning it into your dream home.'

Like they were doing now?

'While training Sentry's new recruits on some nearby piece of land that you've bought that has an insane obstacle course and—' her fingers wriggled in the air as if searching for other things new recruits might need training for '—electronic communication facilities.'

He stilled. That idea had legs.

'Or—' she tapped a finger against her lips '—you decide to part company with Sentry and flip houses for a living instead.'

Working on the villa had been fun, and doing

up a place of his own appealed, but he didn't want to make a career out of it.

'You get your pilot's licence and start flying freight planes to Africa or Asia, learn a new language…play basketball.' She gave a wicked giggle. 'Or you could have a midlife crisis and buy an outrageously expensive status symbol of a sports car and take up with a twenty-year-old showgirl.'

With a growl, he lunged and pinned her beneath him. 'I'll skip the midlife crisis if it's all the same to you.'

'Very wise.'

Her hands smoothed down his back and flanks as if she loved the feel of him, as if she couldn't help but touch him. It was all he could do not to purr.

'Turnabout—tell me what features in your hypothetical future.'

'The fantasy one? The one I'd wish for if I had a genie to grant me wishes?'

He nodded and she grinned and it snagged at something inside him.

'Well, first of all I'd drop out of the media spotlight entirely. However, my interior design business would take off and all the people *in the know* would pay outrageous sums to have me designing their home and office spaces. I'll be so in demand I'll get to pick and choose what jobs I do.' Her eyes twinkled. 'Even The Palace will call me in.'

He chuckled. 'You like to dream big.'

'It's the only way to do it.'

It hit him then that he'd never dreamed big. Ever. He hadn't actually dreamed at all, beyond wanting to get away from his father and wanting his mother to do the same. He'd worked for his father's building company because he'd been forced into it; he'd joined the army as it had been the easiest option open to him; he'd left the army with Sarge and Logan to start a business because it had seemed like the next logical step. But he'd never asked himself what, given the chance, he'd *like* to do.

She cocked her head to one side. 'And I'll continue to support Second Chances, and the charity will gain nationwide prominence and go from strength to strength.'

'Sounds like you're going to be busy.'

'But not too busy to holiday in my Greek island villa whenever I can, because, of course, I'll have made enough money to buy this place.'

'Of course,' he agreed gravely.

Actually, it wouldn't be a hardship to spend more time in this place. He loved what she'd done—what *they'd* done. He had more than enough money in the bank to buy the villa too. Sentry was ludicrously successful. He worked hard but rarely spent the fruits of his labour. He could—

What the hell...?

He shook the thought away. That wasn't *his* fantasy.

'Kids? A family of your own?' he forced himself to ask.

'Maybe not. I've never been particularly maternal. I keep waiting for that ticking clock everyone talks about to start counting down, but so far...' She shook her head. 'And I'm not having kids unless I *really* want them.'

'I feel the same.'

'As for getting married...'

A shadow passed over her face and he knew that she was thinking about Sebastian.

'This is your fantasy guy, remember?' Not some lying, cheating scumbag.

'Okay, then he's someone who isn't the least interested in what my parents do for a living, he's kind—'

'How is he kind?'

'He feeds stray dogs, stands up to bullies, and because he's my dream man he brings me chocolate whenever I'm feeling down. Also, he's really good in bed.' Her eyes danced. 'If I find a guy like that I might be tempted to keep him, although a husband doesn't *have* to feature in my future. I could instead take a series of beautiful men as my lovers.'

He grinned. 'So you're going to embrace your midlife crisis with gusto then.'

And then she was laughing beneath him, and they were kissing... And it was a long time before either one of them spoke again.

* * *

They spent the rest of the week renovating the reception room. In the evenings, when everyone left, the villa became their cocoon—a cocoon where fantasies played out, where he found himself laughing more readily and enjoying everything more.

He savoured the food they made rather than ticking it off as fuel for his body, savoured the buoyancy of the sea when they swam, savoured the touch of skin on skin when they made love.

It became a cocoon where he found himself playing a series of fantasy games with Janie— silly nonsense games like, 'If you could only visit one place on earth where would you go?' Or, 'Who would you most like to look like? Sing like? Be an expert like?'

Something odd happened as he played these games. It was as if the world opened up to him in ways it never had before. Even though he didn't actually want to have the Beatles around for dinner or look like one of the Hemsworth brothers, or sing like Elvis or paint like Picasso, the parameters around him seemed to expand.

And their makeover of the reception room was a triumph. They'd restored the ceiling rose and ornate cornices, while those extraordinary floor tiles gleamed. The fireplace sported a beautiful stone mantelpiece, and Janie had recycled pieces of furniture that had been in the house when they'd first arrived. Sofas and armchairs were recovered in a beautiful woven fabric she'd sourced locally. Coffee and side tables, a desk and an antique dresser were all sanded and oiled. He custom built a bookcase while Darren and Tian fixed table legs and chair arms.

The pastel colour scheme—powder blues, mint greens and salmon pinks—picked up highlights in the floor tiles and ornamental frieze. There were sociable areas as well as cosy nooks. The light pouring in at those big windows, framed with new shutters, had the room dancing with holiday promise. The room was grand and homely and he loved every inch of it.

Their achievement was rewarded the following week when Team Greece were the runaway winners. They were first again the week after as well with their entrance foyer. The desk that Zach built as a centrepiece—a stylistic rendition of a Greek temple—won the judges' plaudits. He'd been working on it since completing Janie's dream bed. Her eyes when she'd seen it had been worth all the hard work.

That was also the episode that aired Janie talking about Second Chances. He still didn't approve of her chosen charity, but he kept his expression stoic.

On screen, Janie introduced the woman who helped administer the charity—Lena.

Hold on, bestie Lena?

'When I was seventeen, I was home alone when an intruder broke into my mother's house in Camden,' Janie said. 'I was doing homework in my bedroom on the first floor when I heard the kitchen window smash.'

What the hell?

'I crept up to the attic and called 999.'

Smart.

'I was terrified, and it felt like forever, but the police came really quickly and the intruder was caught with a bag full of stolen electronic equipment and some of my mother's jewellery that had been lying around downstairs.'

He listened, equal parts horrified and spellbound.

'The thing is, the reason the intruder was caught was because they were so hungry they stopped to eat the leftovers from dinner. The intruder was only nineteen years old.'

'The intruder was me,' Lena said, taking up the story. She explained how she'd been thrown out of home, how her father had refused to hand over any of her ID or ATM cards or her phone. 'I know now that I should've gone to the police, but my father was a Presbyterian minister and I didn't think anyone would believe me. We'd only recently moved to London so I had no contacts. I could've gone to one of the many church charities, but my experience with my father made me... sceptical about those.'

His heart pounded so loud he was sure everyone must hear it.

'I didn't know anyone was home that night. I didn't know I'd scared Janie so badly.' She rubbed a hand across her heart. 'I was sentenced to fifteen months in jail. Two months into my custodial sentence, I couldn't believe that this is what my life had become and I tried to take my own life.'

His gut churned. If he'd had a sister, one living in the same house as him…

Janie took up the thread of the story again. 'When I heard about that, I visited Lena in prison. I couldn't get the thought out of my head that she'd been so hungry she'd stopped to eat leftovers. It didn't fit my idea of a hardened criminal.'

It didn't fit his either.

'And when I met her I realised she wasn't that different from me. We'd just been born into very different families. I'd received all of the advantages while Lena had received none.' Janie paused. 'Sure, Lena had other options; she didn't have to break and enter. But she was young, desperate and scared. Given the same set of circumstances, I don't know if I could've done any better.'

In that moment everything he'd thought about Janie's charity turned on its head. The two women explained how their friendship had transformed them both and how Second Chances had helped Lena get back on her feet. They were engaging, articulate…and the evidence of their strong personal friendship had his throat thickening.

Janie was doing good work and, whether she won the prize money or not, she'd accomplished what she'd set out to do, which was raise the profile of what he now had to admit was a worthwhile charity. There would be industry professionals lining up to work with Second Chances, offering those in need employment and support. And people like Lena, those in desperate need of a second chance, would now get one.

'I misread everything,' he told Janie when they were back at the villa that night. 'I'm sorry. I've been every bit as blinkered as you accused me of being. You're doing great work, Janie. Necessary work. You should be proud of yourself.'

She didn't gloat or say *I told you so*. Her eyes glowed. 'Thanks, Zach, coming from you, that means a lot.'

It was the sound of a motorboat engine that woke him. A glance at his watch told him it was two a.m. Janie's slow, regular breaths told him she was fast asleep. Slipping out of bed, he padded across to the balcony and saw the lights of a little runabout bouncing out on the water. Probably tourists fishing. He started to turn back when he caught the scent of smoke.

It jerked him into instant action. Shouting, 'Fire!' into his watch to Sarge, he gathered Janie into his arms and headed down the stairs, getting her to safety the only thing on his mind.

She blinked up at him in a daze, but startled into full alertness when she smelled the smoke. And saw the direction of the flames. 'Oh, God, it's our beautiful reception room! Quick, Zach, there's a fire extinguisher and blanket in the kitchen.'

The fire hadn't had time to gather much momentum and they had it quickly under control, but if they'd been sleeping in the second-floor bedrooms at the back of the house... His lips thinned.

Janie stared at the scorched wall and ceiling, the burned-out armchair, and her bottom lip wobbled. 'We haven't lit any of the candles in here. The electricals were all checked.'

Sarge appeared, a silent shadow in the doorway, and held up a jerrycan. 'I don't know how the hell they slipped under our guard, but—'

'By boat. I saw it on the bay. They must've been leaving.'

Janie gaped at both of them. 'You're saying this is deliberate?' Her eyes narrowed and her hands slammed to her hips. 'Who the hell is trying to sabotage us?'

CHAPTER TEN

Z<small>ACH AND</small> S<small>ARGE</small> shared a glance.

Janie tapped a foot. 'Come on, out with it.'

Zach rubbed a hand over his hair. 'This may not mean anything, but we've reason to believe that Sebastian is now dating...'

His hesitation cut her to the quick. 'I don't care if he's dating again. I'm just glad he's not dating me.'

'Isobel.'

It took a moment to connect the dots.

Oh! Sebastian and Isobel?

'You're saying...' Her stomach plummeted. 'Sebastian would love to avenge himself on me because, you know, apparently I cost him two years of his life.'

They all rolled their eyes.

'And clearly Isobel wants to win. But deliberately setting fire to a competitor's property seems a bit of a stretch.'

Sarge showed his phone to Zach, and while Zach's expression remained the same she felt the change in him. He took it and showed her the picture on the screen. Her heart sank. 'Sebastian is on the island?'

Sarge reclaimed his phone. 'That footage came through late last night.'

'It doesn't feel like a coincidence, does it?'

'It does not,' Sarge agreed.

Her mind raced. 'I'm not afraid of Sebastian physically. He's a dweeb, never been in a fight in his life. Which is a good thing. As a rule, I don't condone violence.' But if Sebastian was in this room right now, she'd kick him in the shins.

As if reading her mind, Zach's lips tightened.

'If you shaped up to him, Zach, he'd be a quivering, cowering mess.'

'No offence, Janie.' Sarge flashed her a grin. 'But most men would be a cowering mess if Zach shaped up to them.'

She laughed and something in Zach's posture eased. 'He's big,' she agreed. 'And he can look menacing when he wants to. But the fact is Sebastian would be the same if I slapped him. He wouldn't know what to do.'

'He wouldn't hit you back?'

'I'm ninety-nine percent sure he wouldn't. But this—' She gestured at the scorched wall. 'This I can see him doing.' Her hands clenched. 'Zach, if you hadn't heard that motorboat...' They could've died.

Dragging in a breath, she pushed that thought

away. They hadn't died. She wouldn't panic. 'We've no solid evidence against him.'

'But we'll be keeping an eye on him.' Sarge turned to Zach. 'I'm calling in Lee and Ahmed as reinforcements. They can tail him.'

Zach gave a single nod. 'Good plan.'

'There's nothing else that can be done here to-night. I suggest the two of you turn in and try to get some sleep.' The older man hesitated.

'Sarge?'

'I know what's going on here.'

He gestured between her and Zach and Janie found herself swallowing. 'Are you about to say you disapprove?'

'You're both adults, and it's none of my busi-ness. I just want you to keep your wits about you. Keep your eyes and ears open. It looks like some-body wants to win that prize money and they're prepared to go to extreme lengths to do so.' He smiled at her briefly. 'You're in their sights be-cause you're doing such an amazing job here, Janie. We *are* going to keep you safe, but it'll help if you remain alert.'

His praise warmed her. 'Roger that.' She imi-tated the words she'd heard Zach use. ''Night, Sarge.'

With a casual salute he was gone. Turning, she threw herself into Zach's arms. 'Thank you, tough guy, for saving the day.'

His arms wrapped around her, firm and strong.

'Wish I could've caught the rotter before he started the fire.'

'I'll take a scorched wall and a ruined armchair over what could've happened. Come on. Bed. We've another big day tomorrow.'

The team were horrified when they arrived in the morning and saw the damage. A grey-faced Cullen had the cameraman film it. The authorities were called in to investigate. It all took time they didn't want to spare, but Janie was ridiculously relieved they were working outside, away from the smell of charred wood and smoke. Darren and Tian doubled down, working extra hard as if wanting to somehow make amends. It had her fighting back tears.

Maybe it was that sense of camaraderie—of pulling together—that gave the outdoor space an extra sparkle, but between them all they laid pavers and built a simple pergola that ran the length of the villa on the dining room side. They planted ornamental grapevines that would eventually twine around the wooden beams and supports and turn it into a green oasis. Planter boxes and barrels of petunias, begonias and geraniums in bright colours were added and café tables dotted its length.

The *pièce de résistance* would be the tiny alcove created at the far end between the wall of the villa and the garden shed. A sunny three-walled nook that would be surrounded by lattice trailing with jasmine, and with a small fountain splashing merrily at its centre.

'Ooh, look, the final touches have arrived.' Janie gestured to a newly delivered crate. Seizing a crowbar, she pushed it under the lid and levered it free—an action she'd become adept at. Pushing the lid to one side, she reached inside but pulled her arm back with a muffled shout.

Zach was at her side in seconds, Darren and Tian hot on his heels.

'Bitten,' she gasped, pressing her hand to the painful site on her forearm.

Tian knocked the lid completely off the box and peered inside the crate. Darren blew out a breath. 'I don't know what kind of spider that is...'

Zach had started to bind the bite with a bandage he'd magicked out of thin air. Janie peered into the box and swayed. *Oh, God, it was huge. And hairy.*

Lifting her, Zach carried her to a seat in the shade and made her sit while he finished binding her arm.

'It's a tarantula,' Tian said. 'Tarantula venom isn't normally lethal, but can be painful. Worst case scenario is you might feel unwell for a day or two.' His forehead wrinkled. 'This spider isn't native to the island.' His expression grew grim. 'There's three of them in the crate.'

Three!

'You have to go to hospital and get checked out,' Cullen ordered. 'Rules of the show. Health and safety.'

She wanted to argue, but Zach was already agreeing with him. 'Can we turn the camera off now?' she said weakly. 'I really don't want to throw up on national TV.'

Cullen made a cutting action and Zach carried her to the bathroom and held the hair off her face while she vomited. He flushed the toilet, supported her while she rinsed her mouth. Closing the lid of the toilet, he sat on it and drew her down to his lap. 'The vomiting will be due to the shock. I was bitten by one of those a couple of years ago. No ill effects.'

She nodded, taking comfort in his strength. 'Three spiders, Zach. That's not a coincidence.'

'Sarge will start an investigation immediately. And from now on, only I open any deliveries.'

She nodded and tried to pull herself together, but her arm hurt like the blazes and the thought that someone had done this deliberately…

Don't think about that now.

'Okay, you stay and oversee things here.' There was still so much to do! 'Cullen can take me to the clinic and—'

'I'm not leaving your side.'

Damn.

'That's right. Bodyguard. Where I go you go.'

A gentle finger under her chin lifted her gaze to

his. 'Because I'm your friend and I know you're scared, although you're hiding it well, and I'm not letting you face that alone because I care about you. Darren and Tian know what to do. We can trust them to do it.'

She wept a few quiet tears into his shoulder then, but eventually stood. 'Okay, let's go do this.'

Janie was allowed home later that afternoon, after the medical staff were satisfied that she wouldn't have an allergic reaction, but on the proviso she took it easy for the next couple of days.

When it became clear to the rest of the team that she had no intention of resting indoors, they placed an armchair in a shady spot where she could direct operations. She appreciated being part of things. And she appreciated the distraction from her father's overdramatic phone calls and emails, even though she'd assured him ten times now that she was fine.

Zach unearthed a footstool from somewhere and literally made her put her feet up, setting a table to her right and placing her tablet there. Tian brewed her pots of healthful tea from a recipe his mother sent—nettle, lemongrass and liquorice root—and after the first cup she developed a taste for it. Darren brought her sun-warmed figs and a broad-brimmed hat. It meant she was able to watch as their beautiful courtyard came to life even if they wouldn't let her lift a finger.

'I want to take you all home with me when this is done and work with you forever,' she said, blinking hard at the tears blurring her vision.

The network hired a night-time security guard to patrol the grounds in case of further sabotage. And when the team went home in the evenings, nothing was too much trouble for Zach. He cooked and cleaned, refusing to let her help even a little bit. He brought her baklava and chocolate and chilled glasses of ginger beer. He watched her like a hawk.

At night he wrapped her in his arms until she fell asleep. She still burned for him, but when she'd turned in his arms to kiss him, he'd kissed her back gently but then tucked her head beneath his chin. 'Rest, Janie.'

So she had. She couldn't remember the last time she'd felt so taken care of. If she wasn't careful, she could become addicted to this.

A chill chased through her. She couldn't let that happen. This fling was temporary. She wasn't in the market, remember? And even if she changed her mind about that, Zach sure as heck wasn't interested in extending their affair beyond their time here in Corfu. And she was good with that. She swallowed and nodded. She really was.

The realisation that in another month they'd be leaving this heavenly island for good, though, had her heart twisting over on itself.

Stop it!

She was just feeling fragile from the spider bite and the fire. But the bite no longer throbbed, and she'd noticed that whenever the team had a spare moment they worked hard to fix the fire damage. She suspected that in another week all evidence of the fire would be erased.

But every time she thought of leaving, of kissing Zach for the very last time, it sent a hot rush of panic through her. And during the night Zach turned to her whenever that happened, as if some part of him was minutely attuned to her.

He said he didn't do relationships. To hope he'd change his mind would be the height of foolishness.

You didn't think you wanted a relationship either.

She hadn't counted on Zach, though. Meeting him had turned her world upside down.

Once her two-day rest period was up, the team let her carry out the finishing touches. She hung lanterns on the pergola, placed candles on the tables. A mouthwatering platter of cheese and carafe of wine was strategically placed on one table, a bowl of fresh fruit on another, and a throw rug and book draped on one of the benches in their tiny courtyard. She wasn't sure she'd ever been prouder of a project.

When the show aired, anticipation threaded the air in the upstairs room at the tavern. As they watched, it became clear that while some of the other outdoor areas were beautifully finished, their makeover was outstanding. They couldn't keep the smiles from their faces.

'Except there's a serpent in Janie's Garden of Eden,' Mike, the host, said, turning to the camera.

What an earth...? They'd already covered Team Greece's fire and spider incidents. Had the team been keeping something back from her? Before she could ask, the screen cut away to the network studio, zeroing in on Zach's furious face.

'What the hell kind of charity is that?' he bellowed.

Oh, God.

Beside her, Zach stiffened as their fight after the filming of the first episode played out on the screen.

Mike's face appeared. 'Janie and Zach, do you have any comment to make?'

Her brain seized up. 'Well, Mike...' She moistened her lips. 'I...'

'As you can see,' Zach broke in quietly, but all the more authoritative for it, 'I was as blind and narrowminded as Janie's and Second Chances' very vocal detractors were in episode two. I think we all now know what a great job Second Chances is doing and I'm proud to be associated with the organisation.'

'Well, that is the knight in shining armour line we expect of you, Zach, but—'

'If I'm a knight—' Zach pushed his shoulders

back '—it's because I have first-hand experience of violence, especially the kind directed at women. My mother has been a victim of domestic violence all her married life—my father has terrorised her—but she refuses to press charges. Probably because she's afraid for her life if she did.'

Everyone went so silent she could hear the water lapping in the bay.

'My father belongs in jail. He's a criminal. In my mind I've conflated all criminals with the kind of person my father is—the kind of person who believes they have the right to hurt and dominate others. But as we've learned from Janie and Lena, that's not the case. Some people don't have the support networks or opportunities the rest of us are lucky enough to get. They deserve a chance to turn their lives around. I'm grateful people like Janie recognise that and are doing something about it. I'm glad I've had my eyes opened and my prejudices challenged. And if there's anything I can do in the future to help Second Chances, I'll be doing it. And that's a promise.'

The room broke into applause—her, Darren and Tian, as well as the production crew, all on their feet and cheering.

'You can't say fairer than that, Zach,' Mike agreed.

Afterwards, Janie and Zach leaned against the car, watching the boats bobbing in the tiny harbour.

He glanced at her with shadowed eyes. 'I'm sorry that was caught on camera.'

'You were brilliant, Zach. Perfect!' She wanted to throw her arms about him and dance them around the car.

She opened her mouth to tell him how much she admired him and all he stood for, when her heart pounded in her throat and unbidden words threatened to spill from her tongue. Very slowly, she closed her mouth, a wave of heat washing over her. She'd been about to say, *I love you.*

She couldn't love him.

She *didn't.*

Her heart gave a giant kick but then slowed and the heat leached out of her, leaving a new knowledge behind in its place. She nodded. She loved Zach. Of course she did. But what, if anything, was she going to do about it?

Zach dragged a hand down his face. Janie had been through enough. He still worried that she suffered after-effects from that spider bite. And for him to have made things worse for her by having that stupid temper tantrum broadcast…

He deserved to be shot!

'Tell me what you need me to do to fix this.' He'd do anything.

'Zach, you absolutely and utterly just saved the day in there.' She pointed to the tavern. 'We couldn't have scripted this better if we'd tried.

You just described the same emotional arc that a lot of viewers have gone on, but with a more personal element. I—'

He pushed away from the car to stand in front of her. 'You what?'

'You told the world a personal story—a *painful* personal story—to save the day for me and Second Chances. That had to have been incredibly difficult. You didn't have to do that.'

'I wanted to make things right.' He'd had to make them right. Janie and the rest of the team had worked so hard over the last six weeks, and last week Lena had spoken so eloquently about what had led her to commit a crime at the age of nineteen, and how meeting Janie had changed her life. She'd laid herself bare. She'd cried, Janie had cried, and he expected there hadn't been a dry eye in the house.

It hadn't mattered what kind of sacrifice he'd had to make; he'd needed to make things right.

'Thank you.' Taking a step forward, Janie wrapped her arms around his waist and hugged him. His arms went around her as if that was what they'd been designed for. Resting his chin on the top of her head, he breathed in the scent of her shampoo and some hardness inside him melted.

Eventually she eased away. 'Come on, take me home.'

Home? Was that how she saw the villa?

He mulled that over as he drove. The villa felt

more like a home than his apartment in London did. That was just a stopping-off place between assignments.

Things inside him quickened. Could he buy it? During the final episode, the resorts went to auction. He could buy it and start taking holidays, like Sarge and Logan nagged him to. Maybe Janie would like to join him and—

He cut that thought dead. This thing between them would end when they left the island, never to be repeated. If he bought the villa, and came out here for the odd holiday—a few days here, a week there—he could remember all that had happened here, recall the happy memories and...relax.

He might be ready to consider retirement...in a decade maybe. And he might be ready to take the odd holiday. But a relationship? That was *never* going to happen.

Arriving back at the villa, Zach grabbed a bottle of wine from the fridge. 'Glass of wine down by the waterfront?' It had become the norm.

Her answer was to kick the door shut behind her and advance on him. 'For the last four nights you've played the perfect gentleman, ordering me to rest, but I've recovered from the spider bite and tonight I'm having my wicked way with you.'

She took the wine bottle and set it on the bench. Winding her arms around his neck, she drew his head down to hers and kissed him with a needy hunger that flooded his senses with her heat, her scent, and the shape of her. Growling, he lifted her into his arms and strode up the stairs to the master bedroom they'd made their own.

They made love with an oddly fierce tenderness that left him shaken to the core though he didn't know why. The intensity of their lovemaking shocked him and yet he revelled in it too.

'Oh, man,' she breathed afterwards, her head resting against his shoulder. 'That was…'

He nodded. 'Yep.'

They lay like that, not speaking until their breathing became quiet again. 'Can I ask you something, Zach?'

'Sure.'

'It's personal.'

He raised an eyebrow, which made her chuckle.

'Yeah, I know what we just did was pretty personal, but this might be off-limits personal. It's just… You said you don't do relationships. You said it wasn't conducive to your line of work, but lots of people make long-distance romances work. Haven't you ever been tempted?'

He understood her curiosity. He felt the same way—couldn't help wondering how long it would be before she met someone who'd chase Sebastian's betrayal from her mind and have her ready to settle down.

He wanted that for her. His molars ground together. *He did.* She deserved to be happy. It was just… He couldn't imagine any man good enough for her—who would deserve her.

'Ooh, looking really grim now. I'm sorry. I shouldn't have asked.'

He shifted up against the headboard. 'I don't mind you asking.'

She sat up too until they were shoulder to shoulder, pulling the sheet up to tuck beneath her armpits.

He grinned. 'Protecting your modesty?'

She grinned back. 'Just trying not to distract you.' Which made him laugh. He'd never met a woman so easy to be with.

Slowly, though, he sobered. 'I saw what so-called love did to my mother. According to books and films, love is supposed to make your knees weak, but in my experience it's your mind that love makes weak.' He fought back the long-ago darkness that threatened to close around him now, his chest growing tight. 'When you fall in love with someone, you give them the power to walk all over you.'

'Not every love affair is like that, though. In the best relationships the couple are each other's true partner—helping each other, supporting each other, laughing together and having fun, holding onto each other during the tough times and comforting each other. A relationship like that is beautiful, and something to aspire to.'

'Uh-huh, like the kind of relationship your

parents had?' It was an ugly thing to say. The world knew the acrimony of that particular split. 'Like the relationship you had with Sebastian?' He couldn't stop the ugly words spilling from his mouth. Her words had burned through him, making him yearn for something he'd never had, and something he was determined to keep at arm's length.

He didn't *want* the kind of life she described.

He rubbed a hand over his face. 'I'm sorry—'

'So I finally see what the tough guy is afraid of—he's afraid of falling in love and being vulnerable.'

His head rocked back.

She slid out of bed and pushed her arms through the sleeves of her robe. 'I'm going to grab a camomile tea. Want something?'

But she didn't move. Her hands slammed to her hips. 'I didn't have you pegged as a coward, Zach. But here's the thing about being vulnerable—it doesn't have to make you stupid. As soon as my parents' marriage became toxic, they ended it. That was smart. As soon as I found out Sebastian had been using me, I ended it. Unlike your mother, we demanded more for ourselves. I'm sorry that was the example of love you were given as a child, and I'm sorry that's the message you took away from it. But being in love doesn't rob you of choice, free will or brain cells.'

'Yeah, well, I don't see the point in taking the risk.'

'That's what I meant when I called you a coward.' She tied the sash of her robe with a short sharp movement. 'I thought you were the kind of man who'd face his fears, not run away from them.'

Closing her eyes, she dragged in a breath. 'You've been enjoying our interlude here, haven't you?'

'Because it's an interlude!' he shot back. 'Temporary by definition.'

'Can you honestly say you don't want more of this in your life?'

'Hand on heart,' he shot back, slapping his hand to his chest.

She paled. 'Well, I do.'

An icy fist wrapped around him, squeezing the breath from his body. This wasn't a hypothetical. This had become personal for her. Throwing the covers back, he stalked across to her. 'We agreed this was temporary.'

She folded her arms. 'We did.'

'You said this wouldn't mean anything to you.' Her gaze slid away.

'Has this thing—' he gestured between them '—started to mean something more to you?'

He wanted her to deny it. He didn't want to hurt her, but he'd warned her relationships weren't on his agenda and he wasn't changing his mind.

Her chin lifted. 'What if it has?'

He wheeled away. 'This ends now!'

'Is that you attempting to protect me?' She advanced on him, pushing a finger in his chest. 'Because you think you know what's best for me? Well, you know diddly-squat, Zach Cartwright. You're not trying to protect me. You're trying to protect yourself.'

'We're moving out of this bedroom and back to the bedrooms on the second floor. *Now*.'

'Fine with me!' She gathered up her things from the side table. 'One day, when you're no longer working your high-stakes assignments, you're going to look at your life and see all you've sacrificed, see all you missed out on, and you're going to regret it.' She pressed a hand to her heart, her eyes shadowed. 'I fear for you, Zach. I hope something happens to help you see the world differently.'

With that she left and he heard her move up the stairs to her bedroom beneath the eaves. She hadn't made her camomile tea.

Heading downstairs, he made the tea, but when he reached her door it was firmly shut and he didn't have the heart to knock on it. Taking the tea to his room, he set it on the bedside table. He tried sipping it.

But it didn't help. It didn't help at all.

CHAPTER ELEVEN

JANIE WOKE MUCH as she'd fallen asleep the previous night, much as she'd slept—poorly, in fits and starts, and with an ache in her chest that felt as if it would smother her. An ache that threatened her entire life and happiness.

Stop exaggerating. Where's your perspective? Think of Nanny Earp.

Yet it didn't feel like an exaggeration. And Nanny Earp had never denied pain and sadness. They existed alongside life and love and being human.

She loved Zach, but he didn't love her back. It sucked. It hurt. But she wasn't the only person who'd faced this same situation. While it might feel as if the sky was falling, it wasn't. It'd pass. Eventually. Broken hearts healed. *Eventually.*

She rubbed her hands over her face. *What was I thinking?* Not the falling in love thing. She couldn't help that part. Zach might be a big tough guy on the outside, but he had a marshmallow centre. He'd listened to her, cared what she thought, and had tried to make things easier for her. He hadn't bellyached about being stranded in Corfu when he'd have preferred to be somewhere else, doing something else.

Zach might be self-contained, but he was also kind. She didn't blame herself for falling in love with him at all. What she blamed herself for was letting him know.

He'd made it clear he wasn't interested in anything long-term. They could've had two more weeks of hot sex and friendship, if only she'd kept her mouth shut.

'No use crying over spilled milk.' Nanny Earp's voice sounded through her. *'What's done is done.'*

Pulling in a breath, she let it out slowly. Worrying about it, going over and over it…obsessing wouldn't help. And if it weren't for Zach, she might never have remembered that. She might have a broken heart and plenty of regrets, but it wouldn't stop her from doing the job she'd come here to do—to prove what she was capable of, to both herself and the world.

Forcing herself out of bed, she showered and dressed. Girding her loins, she headed down to breakfast. Zach had his back to her when she entered the kitchen, but he froze all the same. The rigid lines of his body had her heart throbbing.

'Right, let's say a few things, clear the air, and draw a line under this forever.'

He set toast onto a plate before turning and

planting his feet. As if getting ready for her to take a swing at him or something. A part of her wanted to weep for him then because *that* was the experience of love he'd had growing up. No wonder he didn't want to take a risk on it now.

'We both know that what's happened here has meant more to me than it has to you. And now you're feeling guilty about that, and probably worried I'm going to make a scene.' She gripped her hands in front of her. That *wasn't* going to happen. 'All of that is a waste of time and energy. So stop with the guilt trips already and I won't throw any temper tantrums, agreed?'

Easing past him, she placed bread in the toaster, stared out of the window towards the pine grove. 'We're both adults. We've a job to do. Let's focus on that.'

'And that's it?'

He wanted more? Her toast popped up. Dropping it onto a plate, she took a seat at the table and reached for the butter and marmalade.

'Unless you have something to say?'

He shifted his weight from one foot to the other, his frown deepening.

'Very articulate.' She rolled her eyes. 'I didn't mean to fall in love with you, Zach. You didn't know it was going to happen. Nobody's to blame.'

He sat with a thump.

'And I'm not going to argue with you or try to change your mind. You're an adult, you know your own mind.' She bit into her toast, relishing the tart sweetness of the marmalade. 'I mean, clearly you have appalling taste turning someone like me down when I'm such a prize.'

He stabbed a finger at her. 'Don't put yourself down!'

She raised her hands. 'It was a joke.' She huffed out a laugh. 'I could have so much sport with you, but I'll refrain.' She ate more toast. 'I'm sorry you're cutting love from your life, Zach. I think it's a mistake.' She was sad for him. She swallowed the lump in her throat, sadder for him than she was for herself. 'But it's your mistake to make.'

A frown etched hard lines on his brow. 'You sound so...*together*.'

'I feel together.' And it was true. 'The thing is...' she met his gaze, refusing to flinch '...broken hearts mend. This isn't the end of the world and I refuse to turn it into the tragedy of the century.'

She'd cry buckets over this man when she returned home, but she'd also get up each morning and go to work, meet up with Beck and Lena, have dinner with her parents. Nothing much would change. Eventually she'd start to date again.

'You've found your internal compass.'

It seemed she had. And she was glad of it.

She dusted off her hands. 'Okay, with that out of the way, can we now talk about the mystery challenge?' This would be their final challenge. Each team would be given a task individually tailored to their property's needs, and two weeks to complete it. 'It's going to be the kitchen, isn't it? They're going to want us to transform this room into a commercial kitchen.'

'Is that bad?'

'Stainless steel benchtops…a brand spanking-new commercial oven…' Her nose wrinkled.

'Blow the budget?'

'More a case of spoiling the charm of the room.' She'd hate to transform it into something so soul-less.

One broad shoulder lifted. 'They could ask us to turn the bedrooms under the eaves into a honeymoon suite.'

'Ooh!' Images fired through her. 'That would be so much fun. Hurry up, finish your breakfast and let's get up there and make some plans.'

She needed to keep busy and she'd work with whatever she had to hand.

'And here is your mystery renovation challenge, Team Greece.' Mike's face flashed onto her laptop's screen.

Janie crossed her fingers and toes.

'We want you to makeover your villa's façade—just the front—and turn it into something that would make people want to stay. You have transformed the interior and we now want to see that reflected in the front of the building. First impressions count and I think we can all agree that at

the moment it's shabby and unloved. Good luck!'
And with that, Mike's face vanished.

'How do you feel about the challenge?' Cullen
asked, the camera and sound men in position. She
and Zach sat at the table under the tree; Darren
and Tian stood behind them.

She hadn't seen this challenge coming, not for
a moment.

'Nervous,' she admitted. 'This is totally out of
my wheelhouse.' She pushed her shoulders back.
'But I have a great team, we still have a decent
amount left in the kitty, and we'll give it our best
shot.'

Gathering around her laptop, they made a plan.

'We need to get rid of the plaster render and
take it back to the original stone,' Zach said.

'It'll make all the difference,' Darren agreed.
'Backbreaking work, but once it's done...'

She glanced at them. 'Amazing?'

'Totally,' Tian said.

Pulling out her phone to make a shopping list,
she said, 'Tell me what we need.'

Scaffolding,' Zach said.

'Wire brushes,' Darren said. 'Lots of them.
And lime mortar.'

'Plants,' Tian said. 'And pavers.'

The suggestions came thick and fast. She ordered
the scaffolding, to be delivered in the morning.

Zach took her phone and glanced down the list.
'It'll be quicker if you and I go and grab this now.'

'Darren and I will begin pulling out the garden,' Tian said. 'We need to make it beautiful.'

'You worried?' Zach asked as they drove to the town of Kassiopi. Their little local village wasn't equipped with all they'd need.

'A bit, but we have a plan, and if we can pull this off…'

If they pulled this off, she might just win a million pounds for Second Chances.

Two hours later, Janie checked their list. 'All that's left are the wire brushes.' This was their third hardware store. All three of them had been out of wire brushes. As if someone had bought them all up, knowing how necessary they'd be to Janie's renovation.

Stop being paranoid.

Zach did a search on his phone. 'There're another two hardware stores within a thirty-minute drive. We'll give them a go.'

'Okay, but I'm parched.' She gestured to the convenience store across the road. 'I'm going to grab a drink. Want one?'

His phone rang. He pressed it to his ear, but nodded at her. 'Sarge, what's up?'

Janie didn't wait to hear what Sarge had to say, but jogged across the road, dodging traffic, needing to take a moment for herself. She might've spoken adult words this morning at breakfast, but too many times today she'd wanted to hurl them to the wind and beg Zach to give them a chance. Her stomach churned. She couldn't do that. It'd be awful for both of them. Not to mention pointless. She needed to remain strong.

Striding past a van, she gave a startled yelp when a hand snaked out and grabbed her and started to haul her inside. She shouted out for Zach, saw the expression on his face as he swung to her before the door slammed shut. A hood was thrown over her head and strong arms banded around her as the van sped away.

Her heart hammered so hard that beneath the smothering darkness of the hood she thought she might faint.

Oh, God. Oh, God. Oh, God.

'Don't panic, Janie.'

The voice that sounded in her mind was Zach's. And the thought that he'd be in hot pursuit helped to steady her.

But Zach had been on the other side of the road. He'd have to turn their van around on a busy road. The kidnappers had a head start. And the number of streets they twisted and turned down had her fighting for air again. Whoever had her captive knew their way, knew where they were going, and they were doing their best to shake Zach from their tail.

The man who held her eventually eased his grip. Dragging in a slow breath, she steadied herself for a moment, before ramming her elbows back into his ribs and trying to smash the back of her head against his nose. He grunted, evaded her head, and the arms around her became steel bands once again.

'Who are you?' she shouted.

Nobody answered her.

Oh, God. Oh, God. Oh, God.

What if it was the person who'd written those vile letters? She lost her mind then in wild panic as she recalled the threats they contained. She fought—tried to bite and scratch and send her head crashing back into her assailant's face again and again. But he evaded all her efforts with an ease that made her feel sick. Finally, she made herself go limp. She couldn't beat him. It would be better to conserve her strength.

At some stage the van finally slowed to bounce down an unsealed road, and finally stopped. She couldn't tell if they'd been driving for twenty minutes or two hours. She was lifted out and carried up steps. A door closed behind her and a lock thrown. She was eased down into an armchair and the hood removed.

Blinking, she stared up at the man standing in front of her. Her jaw dropped. '*You?*'

Zach pulled the car over to the side of the road, slamming his palms to the steering wheel. 'I've lost them!' he shouted with a string of curses.

'I've lost them!' If whoever had Janie hurt her, he'd—

'Calm down, soldier!' Sarge barked from Zach's phone. 'I need you cold and focused. *Janie* needs you cold and focused.'

His knuckles turned white on the steering wheel. Sarge was right. His panic and fear wouldn't help Janie.

'We're going to get your girl back.'

Except she wasn't his girl. Because he'd been a stupid idiot and hadn't realised what she meant to him—had been hiding from his emotions like the coward she'd called him. It wasn't until he'd seen her bundled into that van and driven away that he'd understood all that she meant to him.

Everything.

In that moment he'd realised that he'd settle into quiet domesticity for her—a white picket fence and eight kids, or cats, if that was what she wanted. His high-powered, high-octane life meant nothing to him if she wasn't a part of it.

'Right.' Sarge's voice hauled him back. 'You tracked them to...' He called out the coordinates. 'There's a couple of different directions they could take from there, west or north, but neither lead out of town.'

'If I get my hands on the men who've done this—'

'When, not if,' Sarge hollered. 'And I'll be there to help you tear them limb from limb.'

'*When*,' he growled, holding onto that promise.

'When,' Sarge repeated. 'Because whoever's done this won't have our special forces training. They're toast.'

He wasn't sure he'd ever heard Sarge sound grimmer or more determined. It helped him focus. He and Sarge made a formidable team. They *would* save Janie.

Because any other outcome was unthinkable.

'The smart money is they'll take her somewhere remote, but according to the map it's not going to be too remote.'

Sarge gave him a road name and a set of coordinates. 'Go west until you reach the end and start working your way back. Keep your eyes peeled for the vehicle or anything suspicious. Tully is liaising with the local police and they're tracing the numberplate you called in. I'm sending Lee and Ahmed to search the road to the north. Don't turn your phone off. I want to know your every move—keep talking.'

For the next thirty minutes that was what he did. But with every passing minute the icy hand around his heart squeezed tighter and tighter. *Please give him the chance to tell Janie he loved her. Please give him the chance to grovel and beg her to build a life with him. Let him have the chance to tell her he was sorry, to tell her what an amazing woman she was.*

Halfway through the next thirty minutes he

started making different bargains. He'd give up everything—thoughts of building a life with her, his job, his life—if she was returned safe.

'I have an address. The entire team is on its way.' Sarge called out an address. 'I'll call out directions—I can see you on the map.' They shared a tracking device. 'I need you to stay within the speed limit, Zach. The city is teeming with police. The last thing Janie needs right now is you delayed by getting a speeding ticket.'

He wasn't stopping for anyone, not even the police.

'Or shot,' Sarge added as if he could read Zach's mind.

That cooled his impatience. For Janie's sake he needed to play this smart. He'd curb his impatience, his panic. He'd give into both when they had Janie back safe and sound.

He arrived at the location—a remote but remarkably glamorous-looking farmhouse on the north-western reaches of town. If Janie could see it, she'd approve of the pink stone, the rustic wooden barn and the orange grove. It looked idyllic—as if nothing bad could ever happen here.

He drove into a secondary driveway that Sarge directed him to. It wound behind the barn to the far side of the house where their cars could be hidden behind a grove of trees. Sarge was already there. Zach's nostrils flared when four police cars turned in at the top of the long main drive.

He glared. 'This would've been quicker and easier if the two of us could've gone in there unnoticed and taken the villains out.'

'Agreed, but the mutual exchange of information made that impossible. We'll let them start negotiations, but you and I are getting in there now. Here's the plan…'

But before they could implement the plan, the front door opened and Janie marched out. Unhurt. Unharmed. And he was out from behind the shelter of the trees in seconds.

She stopped dead when she saw the police cars. Glancing in the other direction, she saw him. He kept moving towards her and then she was moving towards him. She started to run. In the back of his mind he wondered when he'd started running too, and then she was in his arms, her arms wrapping around his neck, and he swore he'd never let her go.

CHAPTER TWELVE

ZACH CARRIED JANIE back to the shelter of the trees. 'Are you hurt? Did they hurt you?'

He put her down and started checking her for cuts and bruises.

'Nobody hurt me,' she managed through chattering teeth. 'Zach, I don't want to stay here. I want to go back to the villa. *Please*. I don't want to stay here.'

'But—'

'Nobody hurt me. They had no intention of hurting me. I'll explain when we're home.'

He and Sarge exchanged glances.

'They scared the hell out of me, and I'm *so* angry and I…just want to sit at the table beneath the big tree and have a glass of ginger beer and—'

She burst into tears. He pulled her against his chest.

'Take her home.' Sarge clapped a hand to Zach's shoulder. 'I'll take care of things here.'

An hour later they all sat at the table beneath the big tree—Janie, Zach and the building team,

Sarge and the security team, and the production crew. Janie had eaten and showered and her colour had returned to normal, though her eyes had turned stormy. Which was better than them being cloudy with fear.

She pointed a finger at the production crew. 'If you film or record any of this I'll hit you over the head with the camera.'

The crew rose and packed the equipment in their car, handing their phones across to Sarge for safekeeping.

She turned to Darren. 'Did you know?'

'That you were abducted?' He nodded, his face pinched. 'As soon as it was called in I went on high alert, contacted your father. My instincts were to wait here in case a ransom demand arrived.' This incident had blown both Zach's and Darren's cover.

Something inside her seemed to unbend then. 'So you didn't know Joey Walter planned to kidnap me?'

'He *what*?' Zach bellowed.

She winced and touched a hand to her ear.

'Sorry.' He did his best to moderate his volume, but nothing on God's green could have him unclenching his fists.

They listened in stunned silence as Janie told them how her father had totally freaked out at the twin incidents of the fire and spider bite. He'd been convinced the writer of those letters was behind the sabotage.

'He let those letters get inside his head, and they messed with him.'

They were the kind of letters that could mess with anyone's head, but to kidnap his own daughter...'

Sarge briefly described the letters for those who didn't know about them. When he was finished, Cullen stared at him, horrified.

'When reports informed him that Sebastian had been seen on the island...' Janie trailed off, her lips twisting.

'The idiot panicked,' Sarge bit out.

'He sent Aaron to, quote, *"get me somewhere safe"*. They knew I wouldn't go quietly. Hence the reason for their subterfuge.'

Subterfuge? They'd snatched her—terrified her! Zach's hands clenched so hard his whole frame shook. If Joey Walter had been sitting at this table right now he'd punch him into the middle of next week.

Janie wouldn't like that.

He rolled his shoulders. Okay, he wouldn't. But he'd want to.

'As soon as I saw Aaron I put two and two together, and was on the phone to my father so fast his head must've spun. He'll still be smarting from the blasting I gave him. I made it clear that this time he'd gone too far. I said that if he didn't tell Aaron I was free to go that I'd disown him. And that I'd make that public.'

Good for her.

'He blustered and spluttered until I told him he had until the count of ten to make up his mind. He gave in when I reached eight.' She shrugged. 'Aaron handed the van keys over and I walked out of the farmhouse ready to ring you when police came hurtling down the drive.'

And he'd shepherded her away.

'Joey Walter was amazed we'd traced Janie so quickly.' Sarge looked grim, and Zach bet Joey Walter's ears were burning with whatever well-chosen words Sarge had directed at him too. 'He's agreed to make a generous donation to the local police's swear jar in reparation.'

That almost made him laugh. It shouldn't but... Janie was safe. And that was all that mattered.

She turned to the production team. 'You could make a lot of money if you went public with this story.'

'Not going to happen.' Cullen glanced at his sound and camera men, who nodded their agreement. 'Janie, during filming you've given us all a lesson in integrity, and it's one I'm personally never going to forget. As soon as this show has been put to bed I'm leaving the network.'

She frowned. 'That's a big step.'

'Reality TV isn't for me.' He raked a hand through his hair. 'I don't like this network's ethics.

And I might, um…have some information that's of interest to your security team.'

Zach straightened. 'Like?'

'Antoine is secretly dating one of the executive producers on the show.'

'He's married!' Janie gasped.

'Not for much longer. And his old network will drop him like a hot potato once the scandal breaks.'

Zach glanced around. 'Why?' People broke up and got divorced all the time.

'Because he's married to the network head's son,' Janie said, pursing her lips. 'And with a whole new generation of TV chefs snapping at his heels, he might find it harder to pick up a plum job.'

What a piece of work. Zach raised an eyebrow at Cullen, noticing the way he fidgeted. 'And?'

'One of the writers on a daytime soap told me an odd story recently about being asked to write an ugly threatening letter to be used in an upcoming episode. But the brief was not…on point. And it never did appear in any upcoming episodes.'

The security team all straightened.

'I don't know if it's linked. And I'd have mentioned it earlier if I'd known Janie's situation. I mean, it could be a coincidence, a storyline that was dropped, but it's stuck with me, and when you mentioned the letters Janie received…'

'We don't believe in coincidences,' Sarge said. 'I'll get the writer's details from you before you go.'

Janie stared. 'Those letters were a scare tactic to keep me from joining the show?'

'Could be,' Zach said. 'But until we're sure we'll be remaining vigilant during the rest of the filming. That is, if you want to remain.'

'Of course I'm staying.' She folded her arms. 'I vote we take the rest of the day off, though, and start afresh tomorrow.' Her jaw tightened. 'And we still don't have those damn wire brushes!'

'I have some in the minibus.' Cullen scuffed the ground with the toe of his shoe, not looking at anyone. 'A…uh…contact told me that we might find all of the local hardware stores' supplies non-existent. I grabbed a few before that could happen, just in case.'

Janie beamed at him. 'Cullen, you're a star.'

He winced. 'Just don't tell anyone.'

The production crew left with Darren and Tian. And then the security team left. Janie glanced at Zach, returning from the villa with a tray of fresh ginger beer on ice and some bread and cheese. She recalled the way she'd run to him when she'd emerged from the farmhouse, the way she'd clung to him. She hadn't been able to help herself. She'd thought she'd never see him again.

Being in his arms had helped. It had made her heart rate slow, had meant she could finally let her guard down, trust she was safe. It didn't mean anything had changed between them, though.

With a superhuman effort, she dragged her gaze from the broad lines of that powerful body.

Chin up.

She *wasn't* going to fall apart now. It'd be poor form to reward all of his hard work and chivalry with tears and begging.

No matter how much she might want to. Even if it felt like it was killing her not to.

It's not going to kill you!

Dragging in a breath, she thought about all the movies she'd watched, the books she'd read, the girlfriends she'd comforted through broken hearts. She'd be depressed for a while, would find it hard to have fun or muster enthusiasm for anything, but she'd be fine. Eventually she'd come out the other side. It wouldn't be fun, but she'd survive.

Blowing out a breath, she nodded. Inside she might feel like she was dying, but that wasn't the case.

'What are you nodding about?' Zach slid the tray onto the table, taking the seat beside her rather than the one opposite like he normally did. Maybe he wanted to stare at the view too.

Maybe he just didn't want to look at her.

He poured them both glasses of ginger beer, sliced generous slabs of cheese. She focused on what she could hear—water lapping, the distinctive call of a reed warbler, the rustling in the undergrowth as a gecko searched for insects. It helped keep her agitation in check.

Reaching for a napkin and a piece of sourdough, she nibbled on the bread, focusing on the texture and trying to appreciate it. She could feel the weight of Zach's gaze on her, but she didn't turn to meet it.

'I let you down today, Janie.' The words were softly spoken and all the more powerful for that. 'I'm sorry.'

What the heck...?

She spun to him. 'What are you talking about?'

'I let my guard down. I was hired as your bodyguard and yet you were snatched on my watch and—'

'Yeah, well, as you, Sarge and everyone else *other* than my father knew, the letters were a hoax.'

'We're ninety-five percent sure, not a hundred percent,' he argued.

'And seriously, who could've predicted that my father would do *that*?' She slapped both hands to the table. 'And you did save me. You found me in under two hours. That was amazing.'

He dragged a hand down his face.

'Stop beating yourself up for something you had no control over. Talk to Sarge. He'll tell you the same. Also,' she added before he could argue, 'what would you say to Sarge if your positions were reversed? Examine *all* the evidence—don't exaggerate, don't panic, avoid hyperbole.'

A smile played at the edges of his lips. 'You really have found your mojo again, haven't you?'

She had. Thanks in large part to him.

'The thing is—' he rubbed a hand across his jaw '—I have no objectivity when it comes to you. When you were snatched—'

He broke off, his face haggard, and it made her chest clench. When his gaze lifted, the expression in those blue eyes had the breath catching in her throat.

'It was one of the worst experiences of my life.'

His expression...

She couldn't get air into her lungs.

'I could barely function. All my training... Poof!' He snapped his fingers. 'Gone. The only thing on my mind was following that van and getting you back. Sarge had to bark orders at me to get me focused again, to stop me doing something stupid that would've endangered civilians or had the police on my tail.'

The tortured twist of his lips, the helpless way his hand pushed through his hair, had her fighting the urge to reach for him. He looked... She had to be mistaken. Her heart started to thud.

'What are you trying to say, Zach?'

He shot to his feet, walked down to the shoreline. 'I don't know how to say it.'

She stared at the hard lines of his back, the spasms that passed across it, and ached for him. Moving to stand beside him, she nudged his arm.

'We've become friends over the last few weeks. Good friends. I'd be worried sick if anything like that had happened to you. But seeing me snatched would've reminded you of all the times you couldn't protect your mother, would've raised a lot of bad memories—'

'I wasn't thinking of my mother, Janie.' He glanced down. 'I was thinking how desolate my life would be without you in it. A world without you...' His jaw clenched. 'I couldn't bear it.'

Was he saying...? She had to plant her feet to remain upright.

'I'm struggling, at a loss how to say three little words. Three words I've never said to any woman other than my mother.'

In that moment it felt as if even the tide held its breath.

'Are those three little words *I love you*?' She held her breath too.

He nodded.

She let her breath out on a careful whoosh. 'Why are you afraid to say them? Do you think once you've said them that you'll have to give up your exciting high-powered life?'

He thrust out his jaw. 'I didn't say I was afraid.'

'I'm just working with the evidence at hand.' She wanted to kiss him. 'Do you think if you say those words to me that I'll treat you like your father did your mother?'

His face gentled. Reaching out, he trailed a finger down her cheek. 'You're the opposite of my father. You're a giver, Janie, not a taker. You treat people with respect and kindness. I'm not afraid you'd ever use and abuse me. And for another thing,' he added, 'I'm not scared about changing my lifestyle or my role at Sentry. You've made me see that real life has a lot to offer. Hell, you make me want to join a football team, take up woodworking and find a pub I can call my local.'

Her jaw dropped, hope unfurling in her chest. Zach wasn't talking about them dating between his far-flung assignments and seeing where this might take them, he was talking about something so much more.

She willed her heart to slow. If he was wholly committed to making a relationship with her work...

'Are you afraid I'll throw those three little words back in your face?'

'It's what I deserve.'

'And maybe I don't agree with that, tough guy.'

His chest rose and fell. The pulse in his throat pounded.

She backed up to lean against the table. 'So if you know I'm not going to take advantage of you, and I'm not going to demand you give up your job, or that I'll be unkind or unreasonable, and you know I'm not going to fling the words back in your face and...?' The pulse in her throat pounded like a wild thing too.

'And?'

'And if you really do love me...'

'Don't doubt that for a moment.'

The expression in his eyes told her more eloquently than words ever could the depth of his feeling. She wanted to fling her arms out and dance, wrap them around his neck and kiss him until nothing else on earth existed except the two of them.

Zach loved her!

She had to swallow before she could speak.

'Well, if you know all of that and really feel that way, and I told you it was important for me to hear those three little words... What's holding you back?'

'Important?' His gaze sharpened and he was in front of her in two strides, his hands cupping her face. 'I love you, Janie Tierney. If you need to hear them, I'll say them over and over. It's just that the words aren't big enough to cover everything I feel for you, everything I want with you. I love you with every molecule of my being. I never want to be without you.' His hands tightened on her face. 'A man like me doesn't deserve a woman like you, but I promise, if you'll let me, I'll work hard every day to be worthy.'

He dragged in a breath that made his entire frame shudder. 'I love you, Janie. I love you. And I want you to be my wife, even though I know it's too soon to say that. I want the right to look after you forever—white picket fences, the lot, I'm all in. I'm going to love you to the end of my days and I want you with me until the end of days.' He swallowed. 'If that's not what you want, then tell me what will make you happy and I'll do that instead.'

He stared at her with such naked vulnerability her heart turned over and over and her eyes filled.

'Oh, Zach, that's the best *I love you* speech I've ever heard. I love you too—every bit as much. I want to make you happy. I want to show you how wonderful the real world can be. I want to marry you and build a life with you too—' she gave a shaky laugh '—but I should warn you I'm not all that fond of white picket.'

He stared as if her words were the sweetest music he'd ever heard. 'Janie...'

'Kiss me,' she whispered.

Later, much later, as the sun sank on the western horizon and a pale golden light fluttered behind the sheer white curtains moving in the soft breeze from the French windows of that beautiful master bedroom she'd started to consider theirs, Janie nestled against Zach's side and let out a long slow breath.

'Okay?' Zach asked, his muscles tensing beneath her cheek.

'Everything is perfect,' she told him. 'I never knew I could be this happy.'

'Or that life could be this good,' he agreed, pressing a kiss to the top of her head.

She rested her chin on her hand so she could look up at him. 'What now?'

'We renovate the façade of the villa—brilliantly—and hopefully win Second Chances a million pounds. We return to London, where you'll be inundated with the kind of projects that make your mouth water, while I start a conversation with Sarge and Logan about a new role in the company. When we were playing your hypothetical games and you were throwing around wild ideas for me, one of the things you mentioned was a training facility. I'd like to do that—set one up and run it.'

She sat up. 'You'd be great at that.'

'I never wanted to be stuck behind a desk but that…' He nodded. 'I think I'd enjoy it.'

She beamed at him.

'I won't enjoy it as much as coming home to you every day, though.'

She snuggled down against his shoulder again.

'Your father and I are going to have a blunt conversation when we get back to London, because he's never pulling another stunt like the one he did today. Then…eventually, you and I will move in together. Maybe buy a little place in the country.'

She happy sighed. That sounded wonderful. 'And one day we'll find a pretty little church and get married there when we decide the time is right,' she said.

Placing a finger beneath her chin, he lifted her face to his, his eyes solemn and shining with love. 'I do,' he murmured.

'I do,' she whispered back.

They sealed the promise with a kiss that had their toes curling and a future full of hope and love unfurling before them.

EPILOGUE

Ten months later...

Breaking News!
Renovation Revamp *winners Janie Tierney and Zach Cartwright were wed today in a private ceremony at a stone church in Suffolk.*

Viewers of the reality TV show will remember Janie and Zach not only for their extraordinary renovation of a villa on Corfu, but the remarkable events that occurred during the filming of the show, when two separate sets of contestants attempted to sabotage them.

Unsurprisingly, the guest list didn't include either Isobel Jamison or Sebastian I-Have-a-Monopoly-on-Mediocrity Thomas.

In a surprising twist worthy of a soap opera, however, Antoine Mackay, who did several months' community service at the charity Second Chances for his role in said sabotage, was in attendance. Sources close to the celebrity chef claim he's become dedicated to the charity.

Other guests included members of Team Greece, Tian Tengku and Darren Baker, along with the production crew who were with them in Corfu, including Cullen Brax, who is now the producer of a series of hard-hitting documentaries.

It's reported that the bride wore a designer gown of cream silk and lace, while the bridegroom wore a smile as broad as the Atlantic.

When asked for a comment, father of the bride Joey Walter said, 'I'm delighted to welcome Zach into the family. He's a king among men.'

The couple have embarked on a honeymoon to an undisclosed location. We wish them well.

JANIE GAVE AN excited wriggle as the car passed through a shaded grove of olive trees. 'We're spending our honeymoon at the villa, aren't we?'

'What gave it away?'

Zach flashed her a grin. He did a lot of that these days—grinning, smiling…looking happy. It made her toes curl. Every single time.

'Ooh, the fact we landed at Corfu Airport this morning, perhaps?'

He laughed and her heart expanded until it felt too big for her chest.

Her husband. She still couldn't believe her good fortune that this man was *her husband.*

'But…how?' The villa had sold at auction to an anonymous buyer for a price that had sent the network into ecstasies. Not even the tabloids had been able to unmask them.

He touched a finger to the side of his nose and winked.

Grinning, she shook her head. Of course he, Sarge and Logan had tracked the unknown buyer down. And knowing Zach, he'd have made an offer the new buyer couldn't refuse.

A whole week at their villa… She happy sighed, but it was threaded through with bittersweetness too that it was only for a week.

She pushed the thought away. The next week would be wonderful. A week to make memories they'd never forget. They'd visit the village where people knew them and said hello, asked how they were but didn't take photos of them or invade their privacy. They could go into the tavern where a glass of red wine would be poured for her and a beer set in front of Zach. Or they could head down to the little restaurant on the water and be given a table on the terrace without even asking for it. She couldn't think of a better way to spend a week.

Except spending hot, steamy Greek island nights with *her new husband.*

And speaking of hot... 'Beck and Logan were looking awfully cosy at the reception last night.'

He glanced at her. 'I noticed that too. Worried?'

'I think they're perfect for each other.' She bit her lip. 'Are you worried?' Did she need to warn Beck?

'Never seen him look happier.'

She folded her arms and grinned at the world. 'And Sarge was all puffed up with pride at the pair of you.'

Sarge and Logan had been Zach's groomsmen, while Beck and Lena had been her bridesmaids. As the newspapers had reported, the wedding had been a small affair. But perfect.

'Ready?'

Zach halted the car at the top of the long drive that led to the villa. Her heart pounded. Would it be as wonderful as she remembered?

At her nod, he started down the drive—the lush, well-kept drive—and she gave thanks that the person who'd bought the place made the effort to maintain it. They emerged from the cover of the trees...

Her heart caught. 'Oh, Zach,' she breathed.

'It really is something.' His voice was as reverent as hers.

'Back then, this is the moment I fell in love with the place.' When she'd seen that view. A cerulean sea sparkling in the sun, a rocky shoreline and a pebbly beach. And not a soul in sight.

'And then you saw the villa…'

'And had an immediate reality check.'

Holding her breath, she followed the lush lawn up to the villa, and the tension in her chest released on a puff of warm appreciation. 'It's beautiful.'

He nodded.

During their final challenge they'd removed the pock-marked, discoloured render to expose the golden stone beneath. They'd scrubbed and re-mortared until the façade had emerged, grand in its understated simplicity. The gardens they'd planted ten months ago were now a riot of colour. Scarlet geraniums, pink and white petunias and deep purple violets spilled from the two hanging pots either side of the door.

'It's even *more* beautiful than when we left.' She stared her fill. 'It shows what a difference a bit of hard work and attention to detail can make.'

'And vision. This is all due to your vision, Janie. You put a lot of yourself into this project, a lot of love. And I can speak from experience about the miracles your love can work.'

'Stop it,' she whispered, her eyes filling. 'You'll make me cry.'

Reaching across, he took her hand and lifted it to his lips, pressing a kiss to her palm. 'I love you, Janie.'

She would *never* tire of hearing him say that. 'And I love you. More even than I love Corfu and this villa,' she teased.

Laughing, he pulled her from the car, gave her a kiss that had her blood fizzing, and then gestured at the villa. 'Wanna look inside?'

'Yes, please!' She couldn't wait to see what changes the new owner had wrought.

They walked through the large rooms hand in hand the ground floor, the first floor, and then up to the bedrooms beneath the eaves. She couldn't utter a single syllable.

Back in the kitchen, her mind whirled. Zach took a bottle of champagne from the refrigerator, along with a platter of delicious nibbles. She followed as he led the way back outside to the table beneath the big tree.

'Nothing has changed.' She eased down into a chair, glancing at the tree, the water, the villa. 'It's as if it was sealed up when we left.' As if it had been waiting for them to return to finish the job.

He handed her a glass of champagne, eyeing her carefully. 'Disappointed?'

Slowly, she shook her head. 'I don't want to see someone else's stamp on our villa.' She wrinkled her nose. 'Silly, right?' Because it wasn't their villa, despite the current fantasies playing through her mind.

'I'd like to propose a toast.'

He sounded so serious and formal she rose to her feet. 'And Zach, how could I be disappointed? I'm here with you. It's *you* that makes this special.

We just promised to spend the rest of our lives together. Life couldn't be more perfect.'

The blue of his eyes darkened and it made her breathless in the most delicious way. She waited for his lips to seize hers in a spine-tingling kiss, but he held back.

'I don't know how I got so lucky, because I believe you mean that.'

'Of course I mean it!' How could he doubt her?

Those stern lips softened into a smile. 'So if I were to tell you that the villa is in fact ours— that I was the mystery buyer—and that I had the deeds transferred into your name, that wouldn't impress you in the slightest?'

He was...? He had...? They owned...? Her mind fogged.

Reaching into his pocket, he pulled out a document and handed it to her. Setting her champagne down, she took it, her fingers shaking as she unfolded it. She had to read the words twice.

'We own the villa?' She glanced up, searching his face. 'It's *ours*?'

'Well, technically it's yours. You always did call this place home.'

And he'd bought it for her?

'You wonderful man!'

She started towards him, but he held up a hand. 'Stop.'

She stopped.

'Because the moment you kiss me, I suspect we're not going to stop for a very long time.'

Sounded great to her.

'And we haven't had our toast yet.'

She reached for her glass, feeling as if she had sunbeams pouring out of her.

'Who knows what life will throw at us, Janie.' The expression in his eyes had tears filling hers. 'But here's to a life filled with as much love and sunshine and laughter as we can jam into it.'

She touched her glass to his. 'To a life filled with love.'

They sipped their champagne. He set his glass down. She set hers down too. 'Can I kiss you yet?'

'Please.'

Stepping into his arms, she kissed him with all of the delight and exuberance in her heart. When they eased away long moments later, she held his gaze. 'I love the villa, Zach. But I love you more.'

'I know.' His eyes danced. 'But it's still the best present ever, right?'

She grinned and then laughed for the sheer joy of it. 'Best present ever,' she agreed, throwing her arms around his neck.

As he whirled her around, she swore that somewhere above their heads she heard a Greek chorus singing with unrivalled glee.

* * * * *